Dani

"Nothir~
Independe~
Sugar...Up To A Point."

"And exactly what point might that be, Mr. Randall?" Keezia inquired, her voice like molten honey and her eyes shimmering with a uniquely feminine form of provocation.

"Well..." Fridge's body thrummed with anticipation. "If you were to *independently* put your arms around my neck—"

"Like this?"

"Uh-huh."

"And what if I were to move a little closer...? Are we beyond the point yet?"

"We're nowhere close," Fridge finally managed.

"So there wouldn't be anything wrong with me sort of easing your head down...."

Their mouths met. Mated in an evocative dance that soon became blatantly sexual.

"I want to say that you are one *fine* kisser, Mr. Randall."

"I can do *much* better, sugar."

Dear Reader,

February, month of valentines, celebrates lovers—which is what Silhouette Desire does *every* month of the year. So this month, we have an extraspecial lineup of sensual and emotional page-turners. But how do you choose which exciting book to read first when all six stories are asking *Be Mine?*

Bestselling author Barbara Boswell delivers February's MAN OF THE MONTH, a gorgeous doctor who insists on being a full-time father to his newly discovered child, in *The Brennan Baby. Bride of the Bad Boy* is the wonderful first book in Elizabeth Bevarly's brand-new BLAME IT ON BOB trilogy. Don't miss this fun story about a marriage of inconvenience!

Cupid slings an arrow at neighboring ranchers in *Her Torrid Temporary Marriage* by Sara Orwig. Next, a woman's thirtieth-birthday wish brings her a supersexy cowboy—and an unexpected pregnancy—in *The Texan,* by Catherine Lanigan. Carole Buck brings red-hot chemistry to the pages of *Three-Alarm Love.* And Barbara McCauley's *Courtship in Granite Ridge* reunites a single mother with the man she'd always loved.

Have a romantic holiday this month—and every month—with Silhouette Desire. Enjoy!

Melissa Senate

Melissa Senate
Senior Editor

Please address questions and book requests to:
Silhouette Reader Service
U.S.: 3010 Walden Ave., P.O. Box 1325, Buffalo, NY 14269
Canadian: P.O. Box 609, Fort Erie, Ont. L2A 5X3

CAROLE BUCK
THREE-ALARM LOVE

SILHOUETTE *Desire*®
Published by Silhouette Books
America's Publisher of Contemporary Romance

If you purchased this book without a cover you should be aware that this book is stolen property. It was reported as "unsold and destroyed" to the publisher, and neither the author nor the publisher has received any payment for this "stripped book."

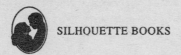

SILHOUETTE BOOKS

ISBN 0-373-76127-9

THREE-ALARM LOVE

Copyright © 1998 by Carol Buckland

All rights reserved. Except for use in any review, the reproduction or utilization of this work in whole or in part in any form by any electronic, mechanical or other means, now known or hereafter invented, including xerography, photocopying and recording, or in any information storage or retrieval system, is forbidden without the written permission of the editorial office, Silhouette Books, 300 East 42nd Street, New York, NY 10017 U.S.A.

All characters in this book have no existence outside the imagination of the author and have no relation whatsoever to anyone bearing the same name or names. They are not even distantly inspired by any individual known or unknown to the author, and all incidents are pure invention.

This edition published by arrangement with Harlequin Books S.A.

® and TM are trademarks of Harlequin Books S.A., used under license. Trademarks indicated with ® are registered in the United States Patent and Trademark Office, the Canadian Trade Marks Office and in other countries.

Printed in U.S.A.

Books by Carole Buck

Silhouette Desire

Time Enough for Love #565
Paradise Remembered #614
White Lace Promises #644
Red-Hot Satin #677
Knight and Day #699
Blue Sky Guy #750
Sparks #808
Dark Intentions #899
*Annie Says I Do #934
*Peachy's Proposal #976
*Zoe and the Best Man #989
†Resolved To (Re)Marry #1049
Three-Alarm Love #1127

*Wedding Belles

Silhouette Romance

Make-believe Marriage #752

Silhouette Intimate Moments

†A Bride for Saint Nick #752

†Holiday Honeymoons

Silhouette Books

Silhouette Summer Sizzlers 1993
"Hot Copy"

CAROLE BUCK

is a television news writer and movie reviewer who lives in Atlanta. She is single and her hobbies include cake decorating, ballet and traveling. She collects frogs, but does not kiss them. Carole says she's in love with life; she hopes the books she writes reflect this. Carole loves to hear from her readers. You can write to her at P.O. Box 78845 Atlanta, GA 30357-2845.

Prologue

Ralph "Fridge" Randall was a man who accepted the existence of Heaven as a matter of faith. Hell—at least an earthly version of it—he was acquainted with, firsthand.

Fridge was a firefighter. A veteran of fourteen years of dedicated, frequently dangerous service with the Atlanta Fire Department. And while he'd readily concede that the vast majority of the blazes he'd battled during this period could be attributed to either accident or arson, there'd been a few that he privately suspected of being, well, essentially *diabolical* in origin.

This was not to say that the only child of Helen Rose and the late Willie Leroy Randall believed the devil was going around striking sparks and igniting multiple-alarm infernos in Georgia's Fulton County. He didn't. Given his awareness that human carelessness, callousness and cruelty often had incendiary consequences, he didn't figure the devil had much need to step in and personally play pyromaniac.

Still. Nearly a decade and a half on the department's front line had taught Fridge that there *were* fires that seemed to be more malignant—more deliberate in their destructiveness—than others. Bizarre as it might sound to folks who'd never gone after a fully involved blaze wielding a ventilating ax or a charged-up hose, there were some fires that just plain exuded evil.

It was such fires that made Helen Rose Randall's son think back to an illustration he'd happened upon in a Sunday-school reader many years before. He couldn't recall the text of the caption, although he was pretty certain that it had had something to do with sin, brimstone and eternal damnation. But the picture…

That he remembered in full-color detail!

The picture had scared the living daylights out of him. He'd taken one look at it and persuaded himself that the flames it so vividly portrayed were intent on his personal incineration. "Intent" as in consciously determined, with malice aforethought.

There'd been no doubt in his young mind about the implications of what he'd seen. Those flames had been out to get him—Ralph Booker Randall—no ifs, ands, buts or possibilities of divine salvation about it.

Fridge had been about six when he'd come across that Sunday-school illustration. He'd spoken about it to only two people in the nearly thirty years that had followed.

The first person had been his mama. Keeping secrets from her wasn't something he'd done as a little boy. It wasn't something he did much as a grown man, either.

The second person had been a fellow firefighter who, despite the difference in their skin color, Fridge had come to trust like a brother. The firefighter's name was Jackson Miller.

Jackson had understood without needing an explanation why certain fires reminded him of the hellish image he'd seen as a kid. Fridge had been sure that he would.

Why had he been so certain? Well, chalk it up to his awareness of Jackson's family history. He knew that there'd been Miller men battling blazes in and around Atlanta ever since Jackson's great-great-granddaddy had volunteered for the force back in 1870. The notion that there were flames capable of transcending the laws of science and taking on a seemingly sentient existence of their own was something Jackson had absorbed at his father's knee.

"Fire's always the enemy in our line of work," he'd observed after listening to Fridge's tale of the Sunday-school illustration and its lingering impact. "But I hear what you're saying, man. With some calls, it feels...personal. Like you're going up against a living, breathing, *thinking* thing that's aiming to get you any way it can. And with those kind of fires, it's not enough to knock 'em down and put 'em out. You need to *kill* 'em."

The warehouse blaze that Ralph Booker Randall faced on the fourth Sunday of the eighth month of his fourteenth year as an Atlanta firefighter didn't feel personal to him. At least...not at first.

There could have been a lot of explanations for his lack of attunement to the situation. Probably the most accurate was that he'd arrived on the scene with a small but significant piece of his mind still caught up with the conversation he and Jackson had been having when the wake-the-dead sound of an alarm had sent them running for their truck.

They'd been discussing the women in their lives. In Jackson's case, a beautiful and brainy Yankee psychiatrist named Phoebe Donovan. In his, a firefighter named Keezia Carew who was as independent as she was exotically attractive.

Different ladies in a great many ways, to be sure. But soul sisters when it came to their capacity for confusing the men who loved them.

"I've said it before and I'll say it again," Fridge had declared at one point, gazing up at the star-spangled sky as though seeking guidance. Things had been remarkably quiet in the nearly fifteen hours since they'd come on duty. While many of the other members of the station's A shift were sacked out in their bunks, he and Jackson had elected to sit outside and shoot the breeze for a bit. "If the good Lord had meant for men to understand women, He would have put the explanation in writing."

His friend and colleague had chuckled briefly then observed, "You seem to understand Keezia pretty well."

"Oh, I understand her just fine when she's on the job, actin' like a firefighter," Fridge had acknowledged with a touch of pride. "But the rest of the time?" He'd grimaced, his memory fast-forwarding through a dozen particularly perplexing incidents. *What does Keezia really want from me?* he'd demanded of himself for the umpteenth time. *Does she even know?* "Give me a break. I feel like I'm stumblin' around in a minefield at midnight."

Stumblin' around in a minefield at midnight...

Strange how that ominous turn of phrase popped back into Fridge's head about fifteen seconds before the first drum of industrial solvent that wasn't supposed to be on the scene blew up, killing a probationary firefighter named Dwight Daniels.

He and Jackson were inside the burning warehouse searching for the twenty-two-year-old "probie" when the blast occurred. They'd just come down from ventilating the structure's roof when Daniels had been reported missing. They weren't the only ones who volunteered to attempt to find him; just the quickest to step forward.

They basically went in blind. The warehouse was filled with smoke. Thick. Dark. Dirty. Fridge knew he'd stink of it for days, no matter how many times he showered.

He tried not to think about what might happen if something went wrong with his self-contained breathing apparatus and he was forced to inhale the rotten stuff. He also prayed that Daniels hadn't succumbed to panic and hyperventilated through an entire bottle of air as probies were wont to do in dicey situations. He'd seen rookies finish bottles that were supposed to last twenty minutes or more in less than half that time. The "huff 'n' puff" syndrome, some veterans called it.

Fridge moved forward cautiously, gripping the steel cable he'd hooked to the outside of the building before he'd started in. Jackson—who was a couple feet to his left—was similarly equipped. As long as they kept hold of their flexible metal guidelines, they'd be able to go out the way they'd come in.

Or so the manual maintained. If the way they'd come in had gone up in flames, they'd have to try an alternate route.

The heat in the warehouse was increasing. Fridge was sweating profusely beneath his heavy turnout gear. His hands were slick inside his gloves. His short-cropped hair and mustache felt sodden. Running his tongue over his lips, he tasted salt.

He suddenly flashed back on something he'd been told early in his training: *The intensity of a fire doubles with every seventeen-degree rise in—*

Ka-boom!

The explosion seemed to come from the back of the warehouse. The unexpectedness of it more than its percussive force knocked Fridge to his knees. Fortunately, the drop wasn't very far. Since heat and smoke rise, the importance of keeping close to the floor was something that had been drummed into him at the academy from day one.

Stay low, you go, went the blunt counsel. *Stay high, you die.*

"Fridge!" It was Jackson's voice. It sounded muffled, but close to normal.

"Okay, man!" Fridge responded, getting to his feet. He did a quick mental inventory of his condition and deemed himself to be shaken but intact. "You?"

"Okay. But I lost hold of my—"

Ka-boom!

This second blast jarred the fillings in Fridge's molars and knocked him flat. His helmet came off. A metallic-tasting liquid flooded his tongue. It was blood. Somewhere in the back of his mind he realized that he'd bitten a chunk out of the inside of his right cheek.

He levered himself up on all fours, scrabbling to locate his headgear. He could feel the outer rims of his ears starting to blister. The back of his neck would begin to barbecue any second. He couldn't see anything. Not a single… solitary…thing.

He hollered Jackson's name.

No answer.

And then the building seemed to groan.

Somethin's comin' down, Fridge thought grimly. He shouted Jackson's name again. He knew that being trapped in a collapse was his friend's personal nightmare. His daddy had died that way. Captain Nathan Miller had been working the nozzle on a water-charged one-and-a-half-inch hose inside a burning frame building when the structure had kicked out and come crashing down. He'd never had a chance.

Fridge found his helmet. He clapped it on and started crawling in what he fervently hoped was Jackson's direction.

A moment later, the something he'd feared was coming down actually did. Whatever it was, it struck Fridge across the back and slammed him to the concrete floor of the warehouse like a pile driver. He opened his mouth to cry out but the pain was so great he couldn't muster the lung power to force the sound up his throat.

He tried to move. Shafts of agony spiraled down his legs, slicing along his nerves like knives. His stomach roiled. He was afraid he was going to vomit. Swallowing convulsively, he once again tried to move. Whatever was on top of him shifted. He thought he heard something snap. Pain stabbed viciously at the small of his back.

A moment later, Fridge saw red. At first he assumed it was blood—his own blood—on the inside of his face mask. Then he realized that what he was seeing was the glow of encroaching flames.

He was caught. God in Heaven have mercy, he was caught and he was going to roast like a pig on a spit.

"Fridge?"

It was Jackson. The shout came across a great distance. Or maybe it just seemed far away because Helen Rose Randall's son was losing his grip on consciousness.

"Fridge?" It was a bellow. Angry. And anxious. "Talk to me, dammit! Where are the hell are you?"

"Here…"

Perhaps he said it aloud. Perhaps he only uttered the syllable inside his head. Fridge didn't know. He wasn't certain it made much of a difference.

Another spasm of pain racked him. He closed his eyes, shutting out the sanguineous light from the flames. This fire was starting to feel personal, he decided, with a touch of gallows' humor. Real, real personal.

He didn't want to die. But if his time had come, he was prepared to meet his Maker. He'd done his best to be a good man, to lead a good life. And while it had taken him a long time to do so, he'd been fortunate enough to find a good woman to love.

If only his love for that good woman had been enough to erase the fear he'd seen lurking like a wounded animal in the topaz depths of her remarkable eyes, more times than he wanted to remember.

If only it had been enough to allow her to fully trust him. Enough to allow her to trust *herself*.

"Keezia," Fridge gasped, invoking the name like a prayer. "Oh...Keezia."

One

Four months earlier

On top of all his other talents, the man could dance.

The realization surprised Keezia Lorraine Carew, although she knew it shouldn't have. It wasn't as though she'd never seen Fridge move. She'd watched him on the job—running drills for rookies at the academy, tending to business at the fire station, responding to calls in the field—more times than she could count. Although he stood a strapping six-four and tipped the scales at a solidly muscular 230 pounds, the man was light on his feet. Potently graceful, like a big, black jungle cat. He could be weighed down by turnout gear and breathing apparatus, but he still seemed to…gli-i-i-ide…when he walked. And he had a knack for maintaining a rock-solid rhythm, even when everything around him was falling apart.

She'd watched how Fridge moved when he was off the job, too. It wasn't a sexual thing. She wasn't checking him out or sizing him up. He was a friend, for heaven's sake! More than that, he was a *fellow firefighter*. If she were looking for a man—which she most emphatically was not now and had no intention of doing anytime soon—she'd have more sense than to go hunting for one in the department.

Still. Keezia knew that she'd be lying if she denied she found Fridge attractive. The source of his appeal was something she'd shied from examining except to acknowledge that he was very different from the brothers she'd been drawn to in the past. He didn't strut his stuff. He didn't represent himself as some streetwise stud. He was, in fact, the kind of mama-loving, churchgoing black man she'd once disdained as hopelessly dull. But now...

What could she say? Ralph Randall compelled her interest. Her attention. And the unsettling thing was, he seemed to compel them against her will.

Keezia took a sip of the beer that had been thrust upon her by a colleague when she'd walked into the garishly decorated hall where several dozen members of the Atlanta Fire Department and their families were celebrating the retirement of one of their own. She wasn't much of a drinker, but she knew the drill. If she'd turned aside the brew and asked for something soft, she would have been labelled a wuss—or worse.

Swaying to the irresistibly down-and-dirty beat of the golden Motown oldie that was wailing out of the hall's speaker system, she glanced around at the gathered throng. The mood in the hall was rocking, verging on rowdy. The esprit de corps—the camaraderie—was palpable. Keezia gave herself over to the all-for-one, one-for-all feeling, wrapping it around her like a security blanket.

She shifted her gaze back toward Fridge. He was dressed in dark jeans and a white T-shirt. The dark, loose-fitting jacket he'd been wearing when she'd walked in—late, thanks to yet another problem with the hunk of junk she drove—had been discarded shortly after he started dancing. The T-shirt clung to the powerful muscles of his upper body as though it had been sprayed on. As for the jeans...

Keezia swallowed and shifted her weight, trying to ignore the sudden fluttering in the pit of her stomach.

All right, she thought with a touch of self-directed anger. Okay. So she'd noticed. She'd have to be blind not to. Fridge's jeans seemed to be clinging to some pretty well-developed anatomy, too. The man was just plain *big* all over.

Too big, something inside her warned. Bigger than—

Keezia clamped down on the comparison before it was completed. She took another drink of beer. A gulp this time, not a sip. She didn't even grimace at the lukewarm temperature.

Motown gave way to a classic cut from the Rolling Stones. All of a sudden Fridge was dancing with a flashy young thing who, in Keezia's considered opinion, should have taken a few of the dollars she'd paid to have her hair braided and beaded and spent them on a brassiere. A pair of super-control, jiggle-reducing panties would have been a good investment, too.

And what were those nails she was scratching against Fridge every time she wiggled near enough to touch him? Keezia wondered with a sardonic snort. A fancy manicure was one thing. Men liked a woman who made an effort to appear her best. But bloodred talons that looked as though a girl had been ripping at somebody's jugular vein? Puh-leeze. Those things were worse than tacky. They were flat-out ugly.

Keezia tapped her short, unvarnished nails against her nearly emptied beer bottle. She was disappointed in Fire Officer Ralph Randall, she told herself. She really was. She'd thought he had more sense than to take up with such obvious trash. She could only imagine what would happen if he decided to take Whoever-She-Was home to meet his mama!

That Helen Rose Randall wanted her only child married was plain to anyone with eyes or ears. But she wasn't willing to settle for any old Sally, Jane or LaToya as a daughter-in-law. No, indeed not. Miz Helen was a lady with very definite standards. She'd take one look at—

Little Miss I-Got-It-So-I'm-Gonna-Flaunt-It said something at this point. Keezia decided the comment must have been downright hilarious because Fridge grinned in response to it, his even teeth flashing white beneath his mustache. A few seconds later, he swept his partner into a Michael Jackson-style spin.

The physical dominance implicit in the maneuver made Keezia flinch. The reaction was visceral. Involuntary. She shuddered slightly, her vision blurring, her palms going clammy. A brackish taste invaded her mouth. A part of her started looking for a place to hide.

Bitch! a nightmarishly familiar male voice rasped inside her skull. *You do what I tell you, when I tell you. You think I'm gonna let some—*

"Hey, Keez!"

Keezia started violently, nearly dropping her beer bottle. Blinking rapidly, she drew a shaky breath. She was appalled by what she'd just experienced. While she understood that she could never fully escape her past, she'd thought she was free from the worst of it. It had been months since she'd suffered such a flashback. That it had been something *Fridge* had done that had revived the fear and shame and helplessness she'd sworn she would die before going through again tore at her heart.

"Keezia?"

"You okay?"

"Hey, maybe she needs to sit down."

"Geez, Keez. You're damned near white."

Keezia got herself under control, steadying her breathing and stilling her trembling hands by sheer force of will. She turned to confront a quartet of her fellow firefighters. Two were African-American like herself. One of them was tall, lean and totally bald; the other was short and squat, with biceps the size of baked hams. The third man had buzz-cut blond hair, blue eyes and the beginnings of a tan. The fourth was a wiry redhead whose faintly glassy gaze suggested he was a couple of beers over his limit. All four were staring at her with a combination of uncertainty and concern.

"Sorry," she said, manufacturing a smile. It must have looked less fake than it felt because there was a perceptible easing in her colleagues' expressions. "I was…uh…zoning out."

"You're sure you're okay?" This was from the taller black

man. His name was Sam Fields. He'd been something of a
mentor to Keezia during her probationary period.

"Positive, Sam. I'm fine."

The four men exchanged glances, then apparently decided
to take her at her word.

"Sorry about shakin' you up," the shorter black man said.
"We moseyed over because we didn't think it was right for
the best-lookin' firefighter in Atlanta to be standin' all by herself."

Keezia made a conscious shift into what she'd come to think
of as her sassy-but-classy mode. It had taken her quite a while
to find the courage to participate in the verbal give-and-take
that was an integral part of firefighting life. The habit of speaking up for herself had pretty much been beaten out of her
during her marriage.

The first time she'd finally felt confident enough to crack
back at somebody who was ragging on her, she'd been suf-
fused by a heady rush of triumph. It wasn't that what she'd
said had been so clever. Indeed, it had been pretty lame compared to the "snaps" some of the guys traded. Nonetheless,
She'd said it.

"Funny, J.T.," she drawled, arching an eyebrow. "I've
heard you tell folks the best-looking firefighter in Atlanta is
you."

This provoked a hoot of derision from the blond firefighter.
"Oh, yeah," he sarcastically concurred. "John Thomas thinks
he's a regular Denzel Washington."

"Let's not be talkin' about who thinks what about their
looks, Bobby," J.T. retorted, jutting his jaw pugnaciously.
"And it's Wesley Snipes I resemble, man. Not Denzel."

"*What?*" The man addressed as Bobby gave another hoot.
"Give me a break! You resemble Wesley Snipes about as
much as Mitch here resembles what's-his-name—that guy
from *Backdraft.*"

The redheaded Mitch, who'd started listing to the left,
straightened abruptly.

"*Backdraf'?*" he repeated, slurring the title slightly. "Oh,
man, I *love* that movie! I mean, it's gotta be the bes' movie

about firefightin' ever made in the hist'ry of makin' movies. Y'know? My girlfrien'…she gimme the video of it las' Chris'mas.'' He grinned at no one in particular. "Says watchin' it with me makes her hot."

"You talking about Ron Howard, Bobby?" The inquiry came from Sam Fields, who'd apparently decided that Mitch's inebriated comments were better left uncommented upon. "That red-haired, freckled guy who used to be on *Happy Days?*"

Bobby shook his head. "No, not—"

"You know, Sam," J.T. interrupted, scrutinizing Mitch as though he were a prime example of some new species. "Mitch *does* kind of look like that dude. I never noticed it before. Hey, Mitch. Sober up for a second will you, bro? Anybody ever tell you that you could be the twin of that *Happy Days* guy?"

Mitch gulped audibly, his eyes darting back and forth. He'd clearly lost the thread of the conversation. He opened and shut his mouth several times. Then he belched. The noise seemed to erupt from the depths of his belly and went on for at least a couple of seconds.

"He used to be on another show, too," J.T. continued helpfully, evidently unfazed by his colleague's sophomoric behavior. "Played a little kid. Name of Mopey. Or Dopey. Somethin' like that."

"It was *Opie,* J.T.," Keezia corrected, choking back a laugh.

J.T. regarded her dubiously. "Oh, yeah?"

"Uh-huh. I don't know who Mopey is, but Dopey's a dwarf."

"So? That *Happy Days* dude ain't no giant!"

"I'm not talking about the *Happy Days* dude!" Bobby interjected impatiently. "I'm talking about the guy who starred in *Backdraft,* not the damned director! You know—Kurt Russell."

"You think Mitch looks like *Kurt Russell?*" Sam shook his head and clucked his tongue reprovingly. "White boy, you'd best have your vision checked."

Bobby rolled his eyes. "No, I don't think Mitch looks like Kurt Russell," he snapped. "Geez Louise, Sam. That's the point I was tryin' to make when we got off on this tangent! Mitch looks as much like Kurt Russell as J.T. looks like Wesley Snipes."

"Well—"

"Forget Wesley Snipes, man," J.T. suddenly commanded. "Anybody know the name of the fox who's dancin' with Fridge Randall?"

Bobby and Sam immediately turned in the direction J.T. was staring. Keezia gritted her teeth and looked down at the floor. She knew what was coming. She also knew she was in no mood to contend with it.

"Where?" she heard Sam ask.

"Over there," J.T. replied, probably pointing.

"Over whe—" Bobby broke off, groaning melodramatically. Keezia took this to mean that he'd spotted the "fox."

"Oh, man," he said in an awed tone. "Oh…mama. Will you guys take a good look at that? The last time I saw somebody shakin' like that, it was at my brother-in-law's stag party."

Maybe she should just turn on her heel and walk away, Keezia thought, clenching her hands against her thighs.

"You think Brother Randall recruited her from that Bible class he teaches?" Sam inquired.

"I'd definitely go down on my knees and pray for somethin' like that," J.T. declared crudely. "Ooooh, baby! What I wouldn't give to have—"

"Hey, cool it, J.T.," Bobby cut in, his voice tight. Keezia lifted her head, startled by his abrupt change in tone. The fair-haired firefighter met her questioning gaze for a split second, then looked away. He was beet red. "There's a lady present."

Caught off balance by Bobby's sudden and unsolicited assumption of the role of protector of her sensibilities, Keezia debated what she should do. She'd worked hard to become one of the guys; to prove herself capable of handling all aspects of the job, including the macho horseplay. But the kind of sexual innuendo she'd just heard made her uncomfortable on a number of different levels for a number of different reasons. She knew she couldn't let it pass.

Taking a deep breath, she opened her mouth to say something. Exactly what, she wasn't sure. Fortunately—if fortunately was the right word—Mitch preempted her.

"A lady?" he repeated, glancing around with a bewildered expression. "Where?"

Bobby smacked him on the back of the head, probably a bit harder than he intended. "Keezia, you cracker!"

"Yeah, man," J.T. seconded, sending her an apologetic look. *"Keezia."*

"Keezia?" Mitch turned and stared at her, his mouth gaping open. Then he apparently decided it was all a huge joke and uncorked a guffaw. "Keezia's...not a...lady!" he gasped through his hilarity. "She's a *firefighter.*"

While Ralph Randall was deeply grateful for the kind of upbringing he'd had, there were times when he wished his mama hadn't been quite such a stickler about what she termed "mannerly behavior."

This was one of those times.

It wasn't that he wasn't enjoying his dance with Bernadine Wallace. A man would have to be dead and buried not to appreciate the lady's—uh—charms. Because her charms were abundant. To say nothing of obvious. Very, *very* obvious.

But appreciative wasn't necessarily interested. At least, not interested the way Fridge got the distinct impression that Bernadine—Lord, he wished he could remember whose sister she'd said she was when she'd asked him to dance!—was encouraging him to be. There was only one woman in whom he was interested "that way" and the last time he'd checked, she'd been on the other side of the room, having herself a fine old time with four male firefighters.

He imagined himself handing Bernadine back to her brother—whoever he was—and going over to the five of them. Not directly. Oh, no. He knew better than that. He'd kind of of...stroll...across the floor. Take his own sweet time. Be cool and casual about the whole process.

And once he reached his destination and joined in the conversation, he'd coolly and casually ask Bobby Robbins if he had any pictures of the baby girl his wife had given birth to—what was it? Three, maybe four weeks ago? He might also make a cool, casual reference to J.T. Wilson's recent engagement. Lucinda, he seemed to recall the girl's name being. Word was, she was a real sweet lady. She supposedly was working toward her teaching degree at Spelman College.

Bernadine said something to him. What it was, he had no idea. The volume of the music would have made it difficult for him to catch more than a word or two even if he'd been paying close attention. She apparently thought her remark was funny though, because she punctuated it with a shrill string of tee-hee-hee-hees.

He smiled noncommittally and kept on dancing. After executing a few seemingly spontaneous steps, he maneuvered himself into a position where he could take another look across the hall without being obvious about it.

Two more men—both vaguely familiar—had joined the group. It was like ants to a sugar spill, Fridge thought, his stomach muscles tightening. The problem was, he wanted Keezia's sweetness all for himself.

He'd wanted it for a long time, although he'd spent quite a while avoiding facing up to the fact. And even after finally admitting to his desire, he hadn't acted on it. He'd...well, the plain truth was, he hadn't known what to do.

It wasn't that he was inexperienced with the ladies. Although he didn't do a whole lot of chasing—it seemed disrespectful to his black sisters as well as to himself not to exercise some restraint in that regard—he'd had his share of romances. But when it came to Keezia Carew...

It was different with her, Fridge acknowledged. Very different.

Maybe if they hadn't met in church, with his mama performing the introductions...

Maybe if both of them hadn't been firefighters...

Maybe if he hadn't seen fear in her beautiful, gemstone eyes the first time he'd touched her...

It had taken him close to two years to learn the source of Keezia's fear. He and she had become friends—good, platonic buddies—during that period. They'd eventually reached a point where she'd trusted him enough to share the story of the relationship that had almost destroyed her.

He'd already known that she'd jumped the broom with some dude in Detroit right after graduating high school and that she'd come to Atlanta to visit with relatives a short time after divorcing him. That there'd been some kind of problem in her marriage had gone without saying. Couples did not split up because they were blissfully happy together. But Fridge had never for a moment considered the possibility that this "problem" had involved Keezia being brutalized, body and soul, by the son of a bitch who'd sworn to love, honor and cherish her.

The rage he'd felt after he'd heard her recitation had been more powerful than any he'd ever experienced. It had also shattered the trust Keezia had placed in him.

He hadn't been angry at her in the aftermath of her tale. Lord, no! He'd been murderously furious with the bastard who'd hurt her so viciously. Nonetheless, the realization that he was capable of such violent emotion had shaken Keezia in ways he was still struggling to comprehend.

She'd pulled back from him, her guard going up, her attitude turning wary and watchful. It had become painfully clear to Fridge that the woman for whom he cared so deeply believed—*really, truly believed*—that it was only a matter of time before he turned his capacity for rage in her direction.

What was he supposed to do in the face of that kind of attitude? Fridge had asked himself over and over. Try to defend himself against her fear by proclaiming it unreasonable? Swear by all he held holy that he'd never, ever hurt her?

A fat lot of good either one of those approaches would accomplish, he'd eventually concluded. What right did he have to dismiss Keezia's apprehensions? To maintain that he knew better than she how she should respond to him? Didn't he see that she'd had enough of being told what to do and think and feel?

As for promising to do her no harm—well, Keezia had made it plain that every episode of abuse by her husband had been followed by pledges it would never, ever happen again. Those pledges had been broken, along with several of her bones and two of her teeth. No matter its sincerity, his rhetoric would carry precious little weight when balanced against her real-life experiences.

In the end, Fridge had decided that the key to the situation was patience. He'd earned Keezia's trust once. He could earn it back again. Although her perception of him had changed, he had not. He was still the man in whom she'd chosen to confide the truth about her past. Given time, she would realize that.

And once she did...

He turned, catching yet another glimpse of Keezia. She was laughing, her lush-lipped mouth parted, her slender throat arched like a lily stem. Bold gold earrings dangled from her lobes, glinting richly against her smooth, mocha-colored skin.

She reminded him of the famous statue of that Egyptian queen, Nefertiti. There was such *pride* in her. Such womanly strength. Not for the first time, Fridge wondered what kind of defect would cause a man to try to obliterate those qualities with his fists.

The Rolling Stones' song came to an end amid much clapping and hollering. Fridge turned his attention back to his voluptuous partner. She was fanning her sweat-sheened face with both hands. The polite words he'd planned to utter got lost in a jolt of distaste as he registered the length and color of her fingernails. He grimaced inwardly, thinking about the gut-tearing velociraptors from *Jurassic Park*.

Bernadine moistened her lips and reached for him with one of her red-taloned hands. "You really know how to get down and move," she declared throatily.

"Thanks." He managed to evade her touch without making too big an issue of it. "You shake things pretty good, too, Bernadine."

"You think?" She preened at his compliment, her acrylic nails clacking against the ceramic ornaments in her hair. Then she fluttered her lashes at him. "Tell me, sugar. Do they call you Fridge 'cuz you're cool...or 'cuz you're so bi-i-i-ig?" She stretched out the last word like an elastic band.

In point of fact, Ralph Randall owed his nickname to a little kid. The station where he was assigned was located close to an elementary school and attracted a lot of field trips. A number of years back, he'd found himself knee-to-nose with a kindergartner who'd become separated from his class. The kid had taken a good, long gawk at him and then piped up, "Gee, Mr. Fireman, you're even bigger than my mama's 'fridg-idator!" His firefighting buddies had found this innocent observation hilariously apt and insisted on calling him Fridge from that day forward.

"I—"

A shriek of feedback cut off his response to his companion's deliberately provocative inquiry. A moment later, music started pouring through the sound system again. This time, the selection was a slow, sultry tune. Implicit in the music was the notion that a man and a woman could have just as much fun going at each other standing up as they could lying down.

Bernadine squealed in delighted recognition, practically flinging herself into Fridge's arms. He winced slightly as several of her hair beads bounced against his T-shirted chest like BB pellets. It occurred to him that between her nails and her braids, this woman could do a man some serious accidental damage.

"Oooooh, I love this song!" she declared, wiggling to underscore the point. "Come on, baby. Dance with me."

He could have said no, of course. But he didn't. He didn't because he knew that by his mama's lights, it wouldn't have been mannerly behavior.

Keezia detached herself from the group of firefighters that had gathered around her a few moments after Fridge's partner super-glued herself against him. No one seemed to notice her departure. They were all too engrossed in listening to a story about the comeuppance of a local TV reporter who was notorious for sticking his mike in emergency workers' faces while they were trying to do their jobs and demanding, "Whaddya got? Whaddya got? Gimme something good."

Word was, this jerk had been his usual obnoxious—even obstructionist—self the previous night at the scene of a multiple-car, multiple-fatality collision on I-85. Outraged by his behavior, a stressed-to-the-maximum paramedic had shut him up by shoving something ugly into his hands.

Keezia was just approaching the refreshment table when she heard a girlish voice call her name. She turned and saw a pixie-pretty young blonde coming her way. Following in her wake was a tall, sandy-haired man with sun-bronzed skin and brilliant blue eyes.

The man was Jackson Miller, probably Fridge's closest friend in the department. Maybe his closest friend, period. The girl was Jackson's fifteen-year-old daughter, Lauralee.

"Hey, Keezia!" Lauralee greeted her with a merry wave.

Having been raised in Detroit, Keezia had had a few problems with Dixie-belle accents like Lauralee's when she'd first arrived in Atlanta. While she still found some "Southern-speak" phony-sounding, she'd warmed to Lauralee's drawl very quickly. The girl was as sweet as she was smart. She was also one of Keezia's most ardent fans, regarding her as something of an icon because of her status as a female firefighter and—as she emphatically put it—an *independent* woman.

To say that Keezia had initially found Lauralee's attitude toward her difficult to accept was to severely understate the case. She'd still been in the process of piecing herself back together when they'd met nearly three years ago. The idea that anyone—to say nothing of a sheltered little white girl—would consider her a role model had struck her as a sick joke. Gradually, however, the guileless intensity of Lauralee's admiration had began to get through to her. It had proven a balm for her badly wounded self-esteem.

"Hi, honey." She smiled at the teen, then nodded at her father. "Jackson."

"Evening, Keezia."

"Did y'all hear about the reporter and the paramedic and the chopped-off hand?" Lauralee inquired eagerly.

"Chopped-off hand?" Keezia said frowning. "I thought it was a severed foot."

"Whatever." Lauralee made an airy gesture, dismissing the need to be accurate about exactly which body part had been involved. Then her expression grew serious and she demanded, "Can y'all *believe* people have the nerve to act like that?"

"You mean the EMT?" Keezia used the acronym for "emergency medical technician."

"Oh, no." The teen shook her head vehemently. "I think what he did was wonderful! I'm talkin' about that *awful* TV newsman—" she spat out the name, her wide, blue eyes fizzing with indignation. "Who does he think he is, anyway? Geraldo Rivera? Pokin' his microphone at people when they're tryin' to save lives. Askin' 'em all kinds of insensitive questions. Makes me sick. Why, just a couple weeks ago, he ran his station wagon—you know, that tacky newshound thing they're always promotin' like it was the Batmobile or somethin'?—over a charged-up line at a fire! Now, I believe it's real important to have freedom of the press. But when a reporter does somethin' as stupid as runnin' over a *workin'* hose—well, I don't think he should get one tiny bit of protection from the First Amendment!"

Jackson chuckled and tweaked a lock of his daughter's flaxen hair. "Spoken like the true child of a firefighter."

Lauralee turned, clearly nettled by her father's teasing attitude. "You pretty much said the same thing, Daddy," she reminded him. "And Fridge, too. Remember? Last Monday? When he came over for dinner? He said he'd've liked to take an ax to that dumb old news car and ventilate it, but good."

"There's a rumor going around that the reporter is threatening to sue," Keezia put in, wanting to steer the conversation away from Fridge as quickly as possible. She also knew that Jackson tended to have the inside scoop on departmental doings. No matter that he was only a lieutenant. The man was heavily—and highly—connected.

"He can threaten all he wants," Jackson replied. "But I don't think he'll follow through. There's a videotape of what provoked the paramedic into reacting the way he did, and somebody in the Mayor's office has a copy of it. If the reporter's stupid enough to sue, the city'll release it to all the local stations and CNN. Then the Department of Public Safety will yank his press credentials and cite him for interfering with official business. He might even wind up charged with malicious mischief and reckless endangerment."

Keezia took a second or two to digest this scenario. Although she'd been spared any personal encounters with the newsman under discussion, his reputation was such that she felt justified in detesting him.

"Sounds good to me," she declared. "But what about the paramedic?"

Jackson's mouth twisted. "He's been ordered to get some counseling. He'll probably be suspended without pay for a week or so, too."

"Which is *totally* unfair," Lauralee chimed in with great conviction.

"A lot of things in this life aren't fair, sugar," her father advised, his words infused with a touch of melancholy. Keezia wondered fleetingly whether he was thinking of the untimely deaths of his wife and father.

"Yeah, but—" the teenager stopped, her gaze snagging on something behind Keezia. After a moment she furrowed her fair-skinned brow and observed, "She's still dancin' with him."

"Who?" Puzzled, Keezia looked over her shoulder.

"That woman," Lauralee said in an odd tone. "She's still dancin' with Fridge."

"It's not a one-way proposition, sugar," Jackson admonished. Something in his voice hinted that this was not new conversational territory. "Fridge is dancing with her, too."

Oh, he surely was, Keezia concurred sourly. Why, if he and Miss Bust-and-Braids got any closer, they'd be sharing lungs!

Exhaling a disgusted huff, she turned back toward the Millers. She had no reason to react this way, she told herself. She had no claim on Fridge Randall. His private life was none of her business. If he wanted to go about conducting that private life for all the world to see...well, fine! It was no skin off her backside.

"Daddy says he doesn't know who she is, Keezia," Laura- lee reported. "Do you?"

"I never saw her before." And if she never saw her again, it would be just hunky-dory.

"Mmm." Lauralee shook her head, the corners of her soft mouth turning down. After a few seconds she said, "I don't think he's havin' a very good time."

"Lauralee Ophelia—"

"It was different before," the teen persisted, undeterred by the exasperation in her father's voice. "When they were dan- cin' fast, I mean. Fridge was really into the music. But now—well, just look for yourself, Daddy! You see it, don't you, Keezia? He's all...stiff. It's like he's got a broom handle up his back or somethin'!"

Keezia glanced over her shoulder again. She knew she shouldn't, but she couldn't seem to stop herself. Her pulse gave a curious hop-skip-jump as she once again focused on Fridge and his flamboyant partner.

Maybe...maybe he *did* look a little uncomfortable, she con- ceded after a moment or two. While Fridge certainly wasn't pulling away from his showy lady friend, he wasn't exactly cozying up to her, either. In fact, now that she really looked...well, she had to admit that something about his pos- ture reminded her of the way he'd held himself right after he'd pulled a bunch of muscles hauling a hysterical four-hundred- pound woman out of a burning apartment building.

And then without warning, Fridge's gaze met and fused with hers. Keezia's breath wedged in her throat. Her knees wobbled for an instant. She found herself lifting her hand to check her hair. The crisp texture of her dark, short-cropped curls tickled the strangely sensitized tips of her fingers.

"You know, Keezia," she heard Lauralee say through the hammering of her heartbeat. "I'll just bet Fridge would rather be dancin' with *you.*"

Two

"**D**ance with me?" Fridge asked about five minutes later.

It had taken some doing, but he'd managed to extricate himself from Bernadine Wallace's clutches after the slow, sultry number had finally come to an end. He'd then made his way across the hall, intercepting Keezia as she headed for the door. After an exchange of greetings and some friendly chitchat—keep it cool and casual, he'd reminded himself, cool and casual—he'd issued his invitation.

Keezia tilted her head. "Dance?"

"Uh-huh." Man, she looked prime, he thought. Even better up close than from a distance, which, sad to say, wasn't true with a lot of women. That sweet piece of skin revealed by the modest V-neckline of the loose-fitting pullover she was wearing—*mmm-mmm.* Talk about temptation! And the way the creamy fabric sort of...flo-o-o-owed...over her breasts? Whew! He could *definitely* get accustomed to looking at that.

As for the short, tight, black leather skirt she had on—well, all he could say was that it was *bad,* and with those long, lean legs of hers, Keezia Lorraine Carew was wearing the hell out of it.

"I'm on duty tomorrow," she said, toying with her right earring. Although Fridge wasn't much on women who fussed with themselves in public, something about this unthinking gesture got to him in a very elemental way. He couldn't help but speculate about what it would feel like to have Keezia stroking *him* instead of the burnished metal. "I really ought to be going home."

"One dance." While he didn't want to come on too strong, he didn't want to take *no* for an answer too quickly, either. Although he was well aware that sweet talk tended to put Keezia's back up, he had the distinct impression that this was one instance where she might let herself be coaxed into changing her mind. "One itty-bitty dance and I'll have you out the door right afterward."

"I didn't know you did anything—" his prospective partner paused, and a hint of feminine challenge sparked in her topaz-colored eyes as she lowered her hand from her earring "—itty-bitty."

"Size is a relative thing, Sister Carew," he answered, lowering his voice a note or two and infusing it with just a lick of the resonant bass he turned loose singing gospel every Sunday. "Why, I can imagine more than a few situations when my 'itty-bitty' would be another man's...mighty big."

He recognized that his choice of words was risky. Keezia was unnerved by his size. He'd picked up on that at their first meeting, long before he'd learned the ugly history that lay behind the reaction. Still, wary as she was, she'd decided to start this back-and-forth. He could only hope that she wouldn't decide to end it by reiterating her initial excuse and taking her leave.

For a moment, he was certain that was exactly what she was going to do. Keezia's expression went blank. She seemed to turn inward on herself. Retreating. Remembering. But then she surprised him. Maybe herself, too. The animation returned to her expressive face in a rush. Her richly colored lips parted in a smile that caused his breath to jam somewhere in his chest.

"Mighty big doesn't do a man much more good than itty-bitty if he doesn't know what to do with it," she declared dulcetly. "But let's leave that be, all right? Because if you're serious about dancing with me—"

"Oh, I'm serious," he managed to affirm.

"Well then, *Brother* Randall, you'd better get me out on the floor right now. The song for our one dance just started playing."

The song that allowed Ralph Booker Randall to take Keezia Lorraine Carew into his arms had an insinuating beat, the kind of syncopated rhythm that snuck into a man's bloodstream and started stirring things up. The lyrics had the same sort of sensual hook to them.

Although the urge to pull his partner close was throbbing through Fridge before the end of the tune's first chorus, he disciplined himself not to give in to it. He kept his hold loose, his touch light. While he'd been encouraged by the sexy banter that had preceded Keezia's acceptance of his invitation, he knew his proximity made her uneasy. He could feel it in the rigidity of her normally supple spine. He could hear it in the shallow irregularity of her breathing pattern.

Trust me, baby, he urged silently, stroking gently at the small of her back. *Please. Trust me. I'm not that bastard Tyrell Babcock. I'd never hurt you.*

Gradually, Keezia began to relax within the circle of his embrace. The tension in her slim, sleekly muscled body eased. Her breathing slowed and deepened. The distance between them got smaller and smaller and smaller, then disappeared.

Her hands slid up his forearms and along his shoulders, linking at the back of his neck. The touch of her fingertips against his nape shocked Fridge clear down to the soles of his feet. His nervous system started humming like an electrified power grid.

She didn't plaster herself against him the bold way his previous partner had. She sort of snuggled up close instead, establishing the fit of their bodies by yielding increments. The process was an exquisite form of torture for Fridge, but he endured it without complaint. He was ready to go through much, much worse if it would help Keezia exorcise her demons.

"I was afraid you weren't goin' to make it tonight," he murmured, inhaling the musk-spice scent of her café-au-lait-colored skin.

"Why's that?" There was a hint of huskiness in her voice.

"Well, when the party'd been rollin' for more than an hour and you still hadn't walked in…"

Keezia shifted a little, raising her head and looking up at him. Her expression was difficult to interpret. There was suspicion in it, but it was mixed up with a lot of other emotions.

"You were watching out for me?" she asked after a fractional pause.

He flashed back on that sizzling moment when his eyes had met hers while he'd been slow-dancing with Bernadine. He held Keezia's gaze for a few beats, willing her to remember—and acknowledge—the moment, too. A sudden flaring of her delicately shaped nostrils told him that she had.

"What do *you* think, sugar?" he countered, keeping his voice low.

Keezia recovered her poise with remarkable rapidity. The suspicion in her expression was replaced by a don't-mess-with-me sassiness. "I think you had plenty to be looking at besides the door I might be comin' in through," she retorted with a disdainful sniff.

Her refusal to take the bait he'd offered didn't surprise him. He'd expected her to sidestep his question. But the admission embedded in her evasion—the admission that she'd been keeping tabs on him in the same way he'd been keeping tabs on her—pretty much blindsided him.

"You mean Bernadine?" he asked after a few seconds. Fridge didn't believe in playing one woman off against another. But if a little bit of jealousy helped clarify some of Keezia's other feelings…

"Is that her name?"

"So she said. Miss Bernadine Wallace."

"Somebody...new?"

Fridge controlled the urge to grin, relishing the way his partner was trying—but not quite succeeding—to make her inquiries sound offhand. He suspected that he'd been similarly unconvincing when he'd done his cool and casual routine prior to asking her to dance.

"Somebody's sister," he answered after a second or two.

"*Sister?*"

"Mmm-hmm."

"Whose?"

He shrugged. "Don't remember."

Keezia stared up at him, her eyes flicking back and forth, back and forth. "Uh-huh," she eventually said, her tone skeptical in the extreme. Then she turned her head and leaned her cheek against his chest. She muttered something under her breath as she did so. Fridge couldn't make out the exact words. He didn't really need to. The gist of what she'd said came through loud and clear. Namely, that of all the roles his current dance partner might be inclined to assign to his previous one, *sister* was way, way down on the list.

They danced without speaking for ten, maybe fifteen seconds. Out of the corner of his eye, Fridge caught a glimpse of Jackson Miller and his teenage daughter. They appeared to be having a small disagreement. If the direction in which Lauralee was gesturing was any indication, it involved him and Keezia.

"Why the late entrance?" he finally inquired, wondering uneasily whether his jones for Keezia Carew was a lot more obvious to people than he'd thought. Jackson had picked up on the situation pretty early on, of course. His mama had made a few uncomfortably acute remarks on the subject, too. But aside from them...

No, he told himself. If anybody else knew or suspected how he felt about Keezia, it'd be all over the department. The guys at the station would be ragging him around the clock!

Keezia muttered under her breath, much as she'd done before. This time, though, Fridge caught what he thought was the operative word in her response.

"Say what?" he prompted, wanting to make certain of the facts before he reacted.

A long, frustrated-sounding sigh insinuated its way through the thin cotton fabric of his T-shirt. "I had some trouble with my car."

Exactly what he'd suspected. Should have guessed without asking, in fact.

"The transmission?" That had been the problem the last time, as he recalled.

"Could have been."

"What about the spark plugs?" They'd been at fault the time before last. Or had it been the fan belt?

Another sigh. "Could have been them, too."

Much as he liked the feel of her warm breath fanning against his chest, Fridge figured it was his turn to ease back and make some eye contact. He did so.

"Sugar," he began, gazing down at Keezia. "I know it's pickin' on a sore subject, but that car of yours is one of the sorriest excuses for an automobile I've ever seen. You are in desperate need of a new ride."

"Tell me about it." Her prickly tone suggested that if he knew what was good for him, he wouldn't. "But unless I strike it rich in the Georgia State Lottery, I'm not going to get one till this fall. I want to finish paying off what I owe on my new furniture before I take on any more debt."

Fridge had spent a lot of years messing with cars. Based on that experience—plus his under-the-hood acquaintance with the vehicle in question—he had some major doubts about whether Keezia was going to be able to stick with her very admirable fiscal plans. Not that he intended to voice these doubts at this particular juncture. He didn't. Because unless his ears deceived him, the song he and Keezia were dancing to was going to be over very shortly. He didn't want to squander what was left of it on arguing about how much life might be left in her old junker.

"I'll ask my mama to remember your car in her prayers," he promised, tightening the circle of his arms.

Keezia gave a throaty ripple of laughter. "To tell the truth," she said, letting herself be drawn against him, "I was kind of hoping you'd ask her to ask Reverend Dixon whether he'd consider trying some faith healing on it. I've noticed she seems to carry a lot of weight with him."

"Mama carries a lot of weight with *everybody*," Fridge returned, chuckling. He wasn't just referring to her considerable stature within Atlanta's African-American community, either. Helen Rose Randall definitely believed in living large. If old photographs were anything to depend on, she hadn't just kept her girlish figure over the years, she'd doubled—maybe tripled—it. "But I'm sure she'd be pleased to have a word with Reverend Dixon."

They lapsed into silence at this point, moving in perfect harmony to the last verse of the song and the final rendition of the chorus. Fridge savored the sensation of holding Keezia. It felt so good to him. So…right.

Please, Lord, he thought. Let this last.

The song came to an end. They didn't separate immediately, though. In fact, Keezia seemed as reluctant to let go as he. Eventually, though, she lowered her arms from his neck and started to ease away. While his masculine instincts urged him to do otherwise, Fridge made no effort to stop her. He simply opened his hands and let her step back.

She stared up at him for several seconds, a hint of heat shimmering in the depths of her enticingly exotic eyes. He could see the jump of her pulse at the base of her long, queenly throat. The rise and fall of her breasts lured his gaze for a provocative moment or two before he forced his attention back to her face.

"Thank you," she finally said.

"My pleasure," he answered, meaning it.

There was a pause. Keezia glanced at her watch.

"Well—" she began.

"I'll walk you out," Fridge quickly volunteered. He had a number of reasons for not wanting her to leave alone. Included among them was the fact that they weren't in the safest area of the city.

She shook her head. "You don't have to."

"I know," he responded, clamping down on a spurt of annoyance at her knee-jerk rejection of his offer. He admired Keezia Carew's independence, he really did. He also respected the dark power of the forces that drove her to defend it so intensely. Still, he lived for the day when she abandoned the notion that saying *yes* to a helping hand somehow translated into taking the first step toward inviting a smack in the face. "But I want to."

Keezia was acutely conscious of the curve of Fridge's strong right arm around her shoulders as he escorted her to the entrance of her apartment building about ninety minutes later. The contact was protective without being possessive. There was nothing about it to make her uneasy. Yet nagging at the back of her mind was the painful recognition that protectiveness could be a trap. Accepting it could sap a woman's self-esteem. Make her vulnerable. *Being dependent on a man could be dangerous.* A woman needed to be able to take care of herself.

"I really appreciate your driving me home, Fridge," she said quietly.

"My pleasure." It was the same response—the same inflection—she'd heard after she'd thanked him for dancing with her.

She took a long, deep breath, inhaling the soft, sweet fragrance of the night air. Atlanta had once again had a very early spring. There'd been pansies blooming at the beginning of February, trees budding in mid-March. It was now the second week of May, and Mother Nature was putting on a full-scale flower show. The beauty wasn't entirely without cost, however. Keezia knew that emergency services had had dozens of 911 calls from people thinking they were having heart attacks when their problem was actually an allergic reaction to airborne pollen.

"I appreciate your calling your friend from the garage, too," she added after a moment, slanting a glance up at Fridge. He was a very striking-looking man, with the legacy of his African forebears clearly imprinted on his face. She could picture him in the colorful robes of a tribal chieftain, exuding an authority based on moral strength as well as physical prowess.

You can trust him, something deep inside her suddenly whispered.

Keezia wanted to believe it. She wanted it with all her heart and soul. Her body wasn't averse to taking the leap of faith, either. Not after the dance they'd shared. She could still feel a hint of sexual heat simmering in her bloodstream. It would take very little to bring that simmer to a full, rolling boil.

But wanting to believe wasn't enough. Something deep inside her had once whispered that she could trust a man named Tyrell Babcock, and he'd nearly destroyed her. Until she could be absolutely sure...

Fridge smiled, his teeth bright against his dark brown skin. "Jamal's one of the best mechanics I've ever met. I know some of the comments he made about your car weren't very respectful, but he'll have it up and running by the end of the week."

They reached the front door of her building. Keezia eased herself out from under Fridge's powerfully muscled arm and turned to face him. She nibbled on her lower lip, debating whether to raise the point that had been troubling her since she'd watched Jamal hook her pitiful car to his tow truck and haul it away.

"Jamal was a little hard to pin down when it came to getting an estimate of how much this repair job is going to cost me," she finally remarked, selecting her words with great care.

"He'll give you a good price, Keezia."

That wasn't what she wanted to hear. Well...actually...it probably was, given her limited financial resources. She certainly wasn't looking to get overcharged or cheated by Fridge's friend! But she wasn't looking to be handed some kind of bogus bargain, either.

"It better not be *too* good," she emphasized after a moment, staring directly up into her companion's dark eyes. She needed him to understand that she was dead serious about this. "I heard what he said about owing you for delivering his son—"

"Simone did all the hard work," Fridge interjected with a shrug. The bunch and release of his shoulder muscles was clearly visible beneath the fabric of his jacket. "I just caught Jamal Junior when he popped out."

"Maybe so," Keezia conceded, although she sincerely doubted it. While Jamal Senior hadn't gone into detail, she'd gotten the impression that his son's entrance into the world had been a very dicey matter. She suspected the scenario had been one of those forget-trying-to-make-it-to-the-hospital-this-baby-ain't-gonna-wait types of medical emergencies that every firefighter heard about during training and secretly prayed he or she would never have to face in the field. "The thing is, I saw those looks you and Jamal were giving each other. I don't want him doing me any favors because of you."

Fridge expelled a breath, his features tightening. "Because that'd make you feel like *you* owed *me*."

She stiffened, uncertain how to interpret his tone. He'd sounded—what? Offended? No. Not exactly. He'd sounded closer to…to…*hurt*.

The possibility that she'd bruised Ralph Randall's feelings shook her. The man had been nothing but good to her from the day they'd met.

"Fridge—"

"It's cool, baby," he interrupted, his expression altering with breathtaking swiftness. He brushed the tip of one finger against her mouth. Her heart somersaulted at the feather-light caress. "Forget what I just said."

"But—"

"It's *cool,* baby," he repeated firmly. "I heard what you were tryin' to tell me. I'll explain the way things have to be with Jamal. He'll understand. 'Course, he'll probably end up chargin' you double for parts and labor just to make sure you don't think he and I are conspirin' to do you a friendly turn—but, hey. Sometimes that's how life works out."

Keezia gaped. Was he serious? Was he actually threatening to have his friend stick her with an outrageous bill if she didn't let him cut her a sweetheart deal?

Then she saw caught a wicked glint of humor in Fridge's

eyes and realized he was getting a little bit of his own back. Profoundly relieved, she started to laugh. Her companion quickly joined in.

"Would you like to come up for a few minutes?" she found herself asking as their mutual merriment finally petered out. It wasn't an invitation she'd intended to issue. But now that she had...

"To your apartment?"

She nodded, wondering at the wariness she thought she heard in his voice. "I could, uh, fix you a quick cup of coffee before you head home."

Fridge regarded her silently for several seconds, his dark eyes searching deep into her topaz ones. "You don't have to, Keezia," he said at last.

It was the perfect opening for a retreat from her impulsive invitation. For reasons she was nowhere near being prepared to articulate, Keezia didn't even contemplate the possibility of taking it.

"I know," she said evenly, sustaining Fridge's penetrating gaze. After a moment, she returned to him the words he'd given her earlier when she'd tried to brush aside his offer of an escort out to her car. "But I want to."

There were lots of reasons Fridge accepted Keezia's obviously unplanned invitation. Not the least of them was her coffee. He knew from experience that the brew she served was strong, black and sweet—just the way he liked it.

"Hard to believe this is the same place Jackson and I moved you into last month," he commented, glancing around approvingly. They were sitting in the living room of her one-bedroom apartment in Virginia Highlands. He was ensconced on a comfortable, pillow-strewn sofa. She had kicked off her shoes and was curled up in an armchair angled off to his right. The earthenware mug that had held his coffee sat on a small, tile-topped table in front of him. Keezia's cat, a marmalade-colored feline named Shabazz, was sprawled across his upper thighs, purring contentedly.

"It's coming along," Keezia agreed. Although her words

were modest, they were laced with pride. "I got those—" she nodded toward a collection of shallow baskets hung on the cream-colored wall opposite her "—the other day at that gallery across from the High Museum. Handmade in Zimbabwe *and* marked down 50 percent."

"Impressive," Fridge said with a chuckle, scratching lightly beneath Shabazz's chin. He'd known the cat almost as long as he'd known Keezia. She'd rescued Shabazz's very pregnant mama from a tree during her first week as a probie, succeeding at the task after several veteran firefighters had failed. A month or so after this episode, the mama cat's owners had turned up at her station house with a boxful of mewing kittens. After being assured by her captain that the prohibition against firefighters accepting gratuities did not apply to things like home-baked cookies or helpless, homeless little animals, Keezia had happily taken her pick from the litter.

"You must be wearing catnip for cologne, Fridge Randall," she observed with a trace of asperity after a few moments. "Anybody else comes to visit, Shabazz hisses, spits and scratches. With you..."

"What can I say?" he asked wryly, stroking the cat from head to tail with a slow sweep of his fingers. He glanced down, struck by the contrast between the color of his skin and the color of the animal's silken fur. He repeated the head-to-tail caress several times. Shabazz's purring grew louder with each pass. "I have the magic touch with certain females."

"Mmm."

Something about this nonverbal response caused Fridge to look from the cat to her mistress. Keezia was staring at Shabazz. Or, rather, she was staring at Shabazz being petted. Her gaze was fixed on his hands, the dilation of her pupils reducing her irises to narrow rings of gold. Her lips were parted and trembling. There was a faint flush of excitement along the line of her angled cheekbones. She looked...dazed.

The memory of what he'd felt earlier in the evening when he'd watched Keezia toy with her right earring came back to Fridge. His body tightened in response to an erotic rush of sensation. Blood—heated and heavy—began to pool between his thighs.

Time to go, he told himself.

"Keezia," he said, disciplining his voice into something he hoped approximated its normal tone.

She jerked, causing her earrings to swing wildly, then lifted her eyes to meet his. Although she did her best to hide it, he could tell that she was shocked by the potency of what she'd just experienced. He wondered, not for the first time, whether her ex-husband had been sexually incompetent as well as abusive.

"W-what?" she asked, the word catching in her throat.

"It's getting late," he told her, easing Shabazz off his lap. The cat rebuked him with a disdainful twitch of her tail, then leapt to the floor and padded away.

"Late?" Keezia checked her watch. "Oh. I didn't realize—"

"No problem," Fridge assured her, standing up. "But it's definitely time for me to be headin' home."

Keezia rose to her feet as well, smoothing the front of her pullover with a languid gesture as she did so. The garment's V-neckline dipped for an instant, revealing the top of the shadowy cleft that separated her breasts. She seemed unaware of what she'd done.

Fridge cleared his throat, willing himself to stay focused on her face. "You plannin' to take MARTA to work tomorrow?"

"MARTA?" It seemed for a moment that his hostess couldn't imagine why he'd raised the question about Atlanta's public transit system. Then she blinked, apparently recalling the circumstances that had led to his being present in her apartment. "Oh, yes. MARTA. Absolutely." She underscored the affirmative with a nod. "There's a, uh, bus stop about a block from here. I'll change to the train at the Five Points station. It'll probably be a quicker commute than when I drive."

"Sounds good." His gaze started drifting downward toward her breasts. He yanked it back up. "But listen, sugar. If you should happen to find yourself in need of a chauffeur before Jamal gets your car fixed up…"

Keezia smiled fleetingly, neither accepting nor rejecting his implied invitation. "I'll keep that in mind."

They walked to her front door.

"Thanks for the coffee," Fridge said.

"Thanks for the ride home." Keezia smiled again, less non-committally than before. "And the dance."

"As I said earlier, that was my pleasure." Although he knew it was unwise, Fridge sought to prolong the moment. He made a show of surveying the apartment. "You've got a lot more room here than in your last place."

"Don't I know," Keezia concurred feelingly. If she suspected he was stalling, she gave no sign of it. "That other apartment was so small, I practically had to go outside to change my mind."

He chuckled, dimly registering that Shabazz had evidently recovered from her feline snit and was rubbing up against his left leg. "I have to admit, I sometimes worried the walls might be closin' in on me. I always felt a little cramped."

"I thought about moving the furniture into the hall whenever you came to visit," Keezia joked. "You seemed to get into a lot of elbowing contests with that ugly old sleeper-sofa I had. And you've probably got scars on your shins from bumping into my coffee table. A man your size..."

Her voice trailed off into silence as the blood drained from her cheeks. Her gaze veered off. She trembled for an instant, then went terribly still.

If Helen Rose Randall's only child had been given to cursing, he would have done so.

Neither of them spoke for what seemed like a very long time.

All right, Fridge finally decided, forcing himself to unmake the fists he didn't remember clenching. Let's stop the jiving around and deal with this. The longer we wait, the harder it's going to be to say what needs to be said.

"It bothers you, doesn't it, Keezia," he began, inflecting the words like a statement of fact rather than a request for confirmation.

Keezia brought her eyes back to his. He could tell it cost her to do so. "What?"

"My size."

She made a gesture, obviously attempting to deflect the issue. "You can't do anything about how big you are, Fridge."

He shook his head, unwilling to let her evade the point he was trying to make. "Neither can you, Keezia," he declared. "And I know that scares you sometimes. You've found the guts to take care of a whole lot of business since you left that ex-husband of yours, but when it comes to dealin' with me—"

"What?" She cocked her chin, daring him to go on. "When it comes to dealing with you—*what?*"

Fridge hesitated. Forcing Keezia into confessing her fear was tantamount to bullying her into a corner, and that was something he desperately didn't want to do. He also suspected that it was something she wouldn't forgive.

Carefully, cautiously, he lifted his right hand and stroked the curve of her left cheek. He was attuned to the slightest hint of resistance. Detecting none, he cupped the curve of her jaw gently, finessing her smooth skin with the ball of his thumb. Keezia quivered at his touch, but didn't try to turn away from it.

"Baby," he began, letting his voice drop into a deeper, more intimate register. "Baby, listen to me. I'm bigger than you. That's a fact and neither one of us can change it. But don't you understand? I know what being bigger means. *I know my own strength.* It's been...well, it's been a gift to me. Same as my singing voice. My strength has helped me *save lives,* Keezia. I respect it. I don't use it against people. And I would never, *ever* use it to hurt you."

"I—" Keezia paused, moistening her lips "—know that."

The darting lick of her tongue triggered a snap-to-attention reaction below Fridge's belt. Closing his mind to the pulsing of his flesh he asked, "Do you?"

"Yes." She nodded. "Yes...I do."

It would have been easy for him to accept this assurance at face value and take the next step. Heaven knew, his libido was clamoring for him to do so. But he couldn't. Because with this woman, accepting at face value wasn't enough. Soul-centered certainty was the only thing that would serve in building a relationship with her.

"Maybe you know it up here," he agreed after a moment, touching Keezia's temple. "But here?" He lowered his hand and feathered the tip of one finger against the spot over her heart. "Do you know it in here, baby?"

Keezia released a breath on a tremulous sigh, her eyes wide and liquid. "I can't…I mean, I—oh, Fridge. I trust you. *I trust you more than anybody.*"

The conditional nature of the last statement ripped at him, but he managed to keep his expression neutral. "Which isn't the same as just plain trustin' me, is it."

"N-no." The syllable came out reluctantly, as though she sensed how much her words had hurt him and regretted the pain she'd inflicted. "No, it isn't. But I'm working on that. Only, I can't—it isn't that I don't—" She stopped, closing her eyes. When she reopened them, Fridge caught a glimpse of emotional storm within her. He also glimpsed her determination to weather it intact. "I need…time."

There was a long pause. During the course of it, the dynamic between them seemed to alter. The air around them pulsed suddenly, as though charged by a silent lightning strike.

Keezia's warm, womanly scent teased Fridge's nostrils. The heat he'd seen shimmering in her eyes at the end of their dance was back, more alluring than before. He yearned to stoke that heat to flame. The ignition of the passion he knew she had within her was one form of combustion he didn't fear.

"Is that the only thing you need, Keezia Lorraine?" he finally asked, his gaze never leaving hers. "The only thing you…want?" What *he* wanted at this moment was to kiss that beautiful, lush-lipped mouth of hers. And every instinct he had told him that despite her inner tumult, at least a part of her felt exactly the same way.

Which made the temptation to take the decision out of her hands very, very compelling.

It wouldn't be like forcing her, a voice inside him declared with insinuating persuasiveness. *She isn't unwilling.*

Just…confused. She'd probably be grateful if you made up her mind for her. Isn't that what a man's expected to do? Take a woman's "no" or "maybe" or "I'm not sure" and transform it into a "yes"?

Not this man, Fridge thought with something close to anger. Not with this woman.

"I—" Keezia began. "I—"

"Say it, sugar," he urged huskily. "Say it or show it. This is too important to both of us for me to be tryin' to read your mind."

Keezia blinked as though she were trying to peer into the heart of a dazzling beam of light. Then, with almost ritual deliberation, she lifted both hands and placed them flat against his chest.

The warmth of her palms burned through fabric, skin, muscle and sinew, searing straight to the marrow of Fridge's bones. It took every ounce of self-control he possessed to remain passive beneath her touch. When he thought he could rely on his voice not to betray how close to the edge he was he said, "It's still your call, baby."

Keezia took a deep breath, her eyes searching his. Slowly, she began to slide her hands up the front of his jacket.

The torture Fridge had experienced when she'd fit herself against him as they'd danced had been nothing compared to the torment he endured during the next few moments. The higher Keezia moved her hands, the closer he felt to Heaven. The closer he felt to Heaven, the further he knew he would have to fall if she ran out of trust and pulled back to a place where she felt safe.

Please, Lord, he prayed silently. *Oh…please.*

Keezia slipped her left hand behind his neck, cupping her palm against his nape as though staking a claim. Then she stroked the fingertips of her right hand over his mustache and pressed them tenderly against his lips.

"Kiss me, Fridge," she whispered.

A groan erupted from the very core of Ralph Booker Randall's being. A split second later, he lowered his mouth and did as he'd been bidden by the woman he loved.

Three

Keezia Lorraine Carew was melting like a candy bar in a microwave oven.

"Fridge," she whispered tremulously, marrying her breath to her partner's. She locked her arms around his neck, inhaling his clean, masculine scent. "Oh...*Fridge.*"

He nuzzled at her mouth. She nibbled at the corners of his. He invoked her name on a passion-roughened laugh. She responded with a long, blissful sigh.

He tasted so good! she marvelled, sampling him with an avidity that was more gourmand than gourmet. Forget fine chocolate, fresh raspberries or fork-tender filet mignon. The flavor of Ralph Randall's kiss was finer than anything she could imagine turning up on a five-star menu.

As for the way he *felt*...

The satiny firmness of his full lips.

Oh.

The bristled luxury of his well-trimmed mustache.

Oh, yes.

The gliding sweep of his slick, supple tongue.

Oh, yes...*please.*

"Baby," Fridge groaned deep in his throat, feasting on her as greedily as she was feasting on him. He nipped and licked, suckled and teased. "My sweet, sweet...baby."

She'd wanted him to kiss her, she acknowledged with a pang of emotion. Not friend to friend as he'd done in the past. Oh, no. Forget casual pecks on the cheek or quick, celebratory smooches. She'd wanted him to kiss her exactly the way he was, man to woman.

But this wanting had been tainted by fear. Fear of being rebuffed as too aggressive. Fear of being condemned as too easy. Fear of being tried and rejected as sexually inadequate or worse. So instead of expressing her very real desires—instead of behaving like the independent woman she kept proclaiming to herself she was—she'd retreated into passivity. She'd waited for Fridge to act upon the hungry male heat she'd seen kindling in his dark, deep-set eyes.

He's the man, she'd found herself thinking. He'll make the first move.

She hadn't wanted to be forced into anything. Lord, no! The very idea made her stomach roil and her blood turn to ice. What she'd wanted was to have her fears swept away. Overwhelmed. She'd wanted to be absolved of the responsibility that went with making a choice between "yes" and "no."

To put it simply, she'd wanted Fridge to *take* the kiss from her.

But he hadn't.

There'd been a few awful moments when she'd wondered whether he might be holding back because he wanted her to beg. Her ex-husband had been big on begging. Tyrell had gotten off on bringing her—his woman, his wife—to her knees. And she, stupidly in love, desperately desiring to please, had bought into his mind games. She'd let self-abasement become her natural posture during the course of their relationship.

On some occasions, her groveling had earned her a kiss or a compliment. On many others, the response had been a kick, a cuff or the cold shoulder. Looking back, it was difficult for her to say which of these reactions had been the hardest to endure. The cruelties had been bad. But the kindnesses...

What was there to say? The kindnesses had kept her hooked on Tyrell. They'd also kept her hoping that things would get better.

It was a soul-chilling thing to consider, but had she stayed in her marriage, the "kindnesses" probably would have helped kill her.

"Is that the only thing you need, Keezia Lorraine?" Fridge had asked her a few minutes before, staring steadily into her eyes. *"The only thing you...want?"*

"I—" The words had clotted in her throat as she'd felt the patterns of the past reassert themselves. She'd tried to struggle clear of them. This isn't Tyrell, she'd told herself. Tyrell needed a woman at his feet to feel like a man. Ralph Randall doesn't. "I—"

"Say it, sugar," Fridge had urged, his inflection as imploring as it was imperative. *"Say it or show it. This is too important to both of us for me to be tryin' to read your mind."*

Strangely, showing what she wanted had proven easier than saying it. The potency of Fridge's virile response to her touch had aroused her courage. The tender sincerity in his voice when he'd affirmed that she was the one in control of the situation had emboldened her even more.

At last, she'd uttered the words.

"Kiss me, Fridge," she'd whispered.

She angled her head to one side, enticing her partner with the promise of a more intimate access to her mouth. Fridge accepted what she was offering without hesitation, reciprocating the pleasure he received in equal measure. She shivered as he deepened the kiss, her fingers spasming involuntarily against the toned flesh of his broad shoulders.

The possessive stroke of Fridge's big, bold hands down her back triggered another shiver. It quickly escalated into a voluptuous shudder of response. A moment later, Keezia felt the cup of his palms and the curve of his splayed fingers against her leather-skirted bottom. She went up on her toes as he drew her against the rock-hard evidence of the need she'd evoked in him. She arched closer, the aching tips of her breasts puckering against the restraint of her lace-trimmed bra. Her head started to spin.

"Fridge…"

"Keezia…"

How long the kiss lasted, she couldn't calculate. But it was of sufficient duration to get her hot, bothered and breathing very hard before Fridge finally brought it to an end.

"Enough," he said on a throttled groan, lifting his mouth from hers with palpable reluctance.

"What?" she demanded raggedly, stroking her hands down his chest. Her intention was to pull his T-shirt free of his jeans and push it up his torso. She wanted to feel his naked skin against her palms. So smooth. So warm. So richly brown.

"Please, baby." Fridge trapped her questing, slender-fingered hands between his much bigger ones. His clasp was firm but gentle; the grip of a physically powerful man who did, indeed, know his own strength. "We've got to stop."

She went absolutely still, staring anxiously up into his short-lashed, heavy-lidded eyes. His face was lightly sheened with perspiration. His expression was stark with stress. She'd done something wrong, she decided with a painfully familiar touch of panic. Somehow, some way, she'd failed to please him.

"S-stop?" she repeated, nearly choking on the word.

Fridge nodded, the tension in his distinctively molded features clearly revealing the effort he was expending to keep himself in check. A frisson of alarm skittered up Keezia's spine as she'd wondered how long his control would last. The turbulence of the emotion beneath his restraint was obvious.

"You've got a 7:00 a.m. roll call to answer tomorrow, sugar," he said quietly.

She blinked, confused by this seeming non sequitur. "So?"

"So—" Fridge released her hands and took a step back "—we shouldn't be startin' something we don't have time to finish."

Keezia shook her head, struggling to comprehend the point he was trying to make. It isn't even midnight! she thought.

What in heaven's name could the two of them start now that they wouldn't have time to—

Her imagination kicked in with a synapse-scorching answer before she completed the question. A provocative series of scenes began flickering across her mind's eye.

She and Fridge.

Kissing.

Caressing.

Baring themselves to each other, body and soul. Confiding their most intimate desires and deepest needs.

She and Fridge.

Joining together, two becoming one. Making love as though they were never going to stop, never going to get enough, never going to...

She felt herself flush from the soles of her shoeless feet to the roots of her dark, short-cropped hair as the images inside her head went from erotic to explicit. Her nervous system teetered on the verge of a sensation overload.

"My God, Fridge," she blurted out. "Exactly how long do you figure we'd need?"

There was a short, stunned silence. Keezia spent most of it wishing she could sink through the floor and permanently disappear. How could she have asked such a question? Ralph Booker Randall was a good, decent man and she'd just come on to him like some kind of no-class piece of—

Her companion started to smile. Keezia exhaled in a rush, her heart somersaulting within her breast. The slow curving of Fridge's full lips was just about the sexiest thing she'd ever seen. It was also one of the most reassuring.

"I'm not figurin' 'exactlys' at this point, Keezia," he said, his voice stroking her like a plush velvet glove. "What I *do* figure is that we have a lot of things to find out about each other and we shouldn't rush the job."

Fridge's words touched her in ways she couldn't begin to articulate, reaching deep within her consciousness and resonating at a very visceral level. She caught her lower lip between her teeth, suddenly remembering her earlier statement about attempting to regain the capacity to share herself with another human being without holding anything back.

"I trust you more than anybody," she'd said.

"Which isn't the same as just plain trustin' me, is it," Fridge had responded in an even voice.

"N-no." It had been difficult to say the word. Although he'd disguised his reaction well, she knew her strings-attached assertion had hurt him. A faint tightening of his striking features had given his pain away. "No, it isn't. But I'm working on that. Only, I can't—it isn't that I don't—"

She'd paused, closing her eyes as she tried to settle her desperately off-kilter emotions. She drew hard upon the lessons she'd learned in the three years since she'd broken the cycle of abuse that had imprisoned her and begun to reclaim her life. Finally, steadied by the knowledge that she'd found ways of surviving where many others had shattered, she had reopened her eyes and concluded, "I need...time."

"Time," she repeated, almost to herself. Then she tilted her chin and stared up into Fridge's face. She let her gaze move from his sensuous lips to his broad, strong-nostriled nose, to his expressive, espresso-brown eyes. "Maybe we... both...need it."

Her friend and fellow firefighter lifted his right hand and traced the shape of her left cheek with exquisite care. His touch made Keezia feel utterly vulnerable, yet absolutely safe.

"No maybes about it, sugar," he said with devastating simplicity.

Consciousness didn't dawn on Keezia the following morning. It clouted her squarely in the skull.

"*—Day here in Atlanta! It's now 5:00 a.m.! Time to check in with—*"

She heaved up, smacked the snooze button on her clock radio, then collapsed against her mattress with a muffled oath. When her jerked-awake brain settled to the point of being able to formulate a semicoherent thought, she began taking stock of her condition.

The results were not particularly encouraging. Her hands

were trembling violently. Her pulse was racing like an amphetamine-crazed bunny rabbit's. She was also hyperventilating worse than she remembered doing during her first post-academy call. Ready to rise, shine and fight fires she definitely was not.

"Well, *damn,* girl..." she chastised herself. Rolling over onto her back, she stared up at the stuccoed ceiling of her bedroom and made a concentrated effort to control her respiration. It took some doing, but physiology eventually succumbed to force of will. By the time she had her breathing slowed to something approaching its normal rhythm, her heart rate had decelerated out of cardiac-arrest range and her hands were lying quiescent against her rumpled, floral-patterned sheets.

Common sense told Keezia that she could not have spent the entire night dreaming about the passionate embrace she'd shared with Ralph Randall. But the rucked-up condition of the bed linen—not to mention the carnal throbbing at the juncture of her faintly dampened thighs—argued otherwise. They strongly suggested that her subconscious had been replaying the interlude over and over and over, priming her long-deprived body for additional pleasures and the ultimate release.

Keezia exhaled on a shaky sigh and shifted her position. After a second or so, she lifted her left hand and touched her mouth. It felt warm and full and faintly unfamiliar. An experimental lick of her tongue across the surface of her lower lip picked up a flavor that was not her own.

"Fridge," she whispered, seeming to taste the essence of the man as she uttered his nickname. Shifting her position again, she closed her eyes. She was acutely aware of the teasing brush of the bed linen against her tightly furled nipples. "Oh, Fri—"

Thud.

The sudden compression of her chest by what felt like a dropped bowling ball jolted Keezia out of her erotic reverie. She opened her eyes.

"Meeeee-row," Shabazz greeted her, showing a set of sharp

white teeth and a pale pink tongue. She scrutinized Keezia disdainfully for several seconds, then began to clean herself with haughty precision.

Keezia's overstimulated brain responded to her pet's grooming routine by producing the mental image of long, dark fingers stroking through marmalade-colored fur. The fur metamorphosed into café-au-lait-colored skin. The stroking slowed, altering from soothing to seductive. Keezia trembled, feeling the tips of her breasts stiffen. Something deep within her clenched like a fist then released on a rush of sweet, liquid heat. She tensed, trying to hold back a moan of response.

God. It had been so long since she'd—

Shabazz yowled. She arched her back, glaring at Keezia with predatory amber-green eyes. Then, with what appeared to be a feline version of malice aforethought, she unsheathed her claws and dug in.

"Ow!" Keezia exclaimed, protesting the attack on her tender flesh. She managed to detach her pet and struggled awkwardly to a sitting position. "Who do you think you are?" she demanded of her cat. "That Bernadine What's-Her-Booty?"

Shabazz wriggled out of Keezia's grasp with an indignant hiss. She scampered to the foot of the bed and jumped off, landing noiselessly on the carpeted floor.

"Shabazz—"

"It's now fifteen minutes past the hour of five!" an inhumanly cheerful voice blared out. "Let's check the latest—"

Keezia slammed the clock radio again, hitting the off button rather than the snooze bar this time. She gave herself a few moments to collect herself, then did what any sexually-revved, sleep-deprived firefighter with a seven a.m. roll call to answer would do.

First she kicked off the sheets and staggered out of bed.

Then she stumbled into the bathroom and took a freezing cold shower.

* * *

"Hey, Keezia," a familiar male voice said several hours later. There was a hint of hesitation in the greeting, as though its speaker was uncertain how it—and he—might be received.

Pausing in the act of refilling the station's coffeemaker, Keezia slanted a glance to her left. The redheaded firefighter who'd challenged her status as a lady during the previous evening's retirement bash was standing a foot or so away.

"Hey, Mitch," she said mildly, then returned her attention to the task at hand. She was her crew's designated coffee maker. This wasn't because she was the group's only female, however. No, she'd been asked to do the job because her coffee was acknowledged to be far superior to anything anybody else on the C shift could brew. Given that caffeine was the drug of choice for most of her co-workers (adrenaline ran a close second), this was no trivial distinction.

"Uh, look," Mitch began awkwardly. "About what I said last night—"

Keezia dismissed the issue with a quick gesture. "Over and done with."

"But—"

"Forget it, Mitch."

"I can't." Mitch scuffed the toe of one of his spit-polished, heavy-soled shoes against the floor. "I need to apologize to you, Keezia. I had a few too many beers last night, and I started talkin' garbage. I want you to know I'm real sorry about it."

"You don't—"

"What I said? About you not bein' a lady? That was just plain wrong. Because you are. A lady, I mean. You know it. I know it. Heck, everybody in the department who's worked with you knows it!"

"I appreciate—"

"But you're one of the guys, too," the red-haired firefighter went on doggedly. "Which makes it easy to forget about your bein' a lady. Especially when we're on the job. Oh, I know goin' to last night's retirement party didn't constitute us bein' on the job. At least, not technically. But deep down, considering what it was for and who-all was there, we might as well have been. On the job, that is. And when you combine that fact with all the beers I drank…''

Mitch seemed to run out of verbal steam at this point. But having twice tried and failed to jam a word in edgewise, Keezia decided to make certain he'd finished saying his piece.

"Is that it?" she asked after a moment or two.

Mitch blinked. "Huh?"

"Are you done?"

"Oh." Another blink. "Uh…yeah. I am."

"Okay, then." She spread her hands. "Apology accepted."

"What?"

"I accept your apology, Mitch. End of subject. Case closed."

"You're *sure?*" He seemed genuinely stunned.

"Uh-huh." And she was. She hadn't been insulted by what Mitch had said the night before. She actually considered it an endorsement. Bottom line: *He'd called her a firefighter!*

"Well—"

J.T. Wilson sauntered into the kitchen at this point, flexing his impressively pumped pecs and sniffing at the air like a bloodhound.

"Coffee ready yet?" he inquired, plainly in need of a caffeine fix.

Keezia checked the machine, unfazed by the interruption. Privacy was at a premium in a fire station. That Mitch had succeeded in delivery his apology without gathering an audience was something of a miracle. "Help yourself."

J.T. flashed his teeth. "Don't mind if I do."

She glanced at Mitch. "You want some?"

The white firefighter looked surprised. Then he started to smile, apparently deciding that her offer was meant to confirm her acceptance of his apology. Which, in a sense, it probably was. Keezia did not make a practice of pouring coffee for her co-workers. Brewing the stuff for them was fine. Making like a waitress and handing it around was not.

"Yeah," he said after a moment. "That'd be great."

J.T. took a gulp of his coffee. "Remindin' him you're a lady, huh, Keez?" he needled.

"No more than you're remindin' me that you're a pain in the butt, John Thomas," she retorted without missing a beat. She filled a cup and handed it to Mitch.

"Thanks." He extracted a small container of aspirin from the left front pocket of his dark blue uniform pants.

"Headache?" Keezia asked, frowning. The work she did was dangerous enough without having to factor in the potential risks posed by a hungover co-worker.

Mitch met her gaze for a moment, obviously aware of what she really wanted to know. "I'm okay," he answered firmly, his manner direct but not defensive. "I've had much worse from eating smoke."

"Tell me about it, man," J.T. said feelingly, leaning against the edge of the kitchen counter. "Remember that really dirty arson call we had a couple weeks back? The one off Monroe? I went home with a carbon monoxide banger like you wouldn't believe after that one. I thought my damn skull was gonna crack open!"

Keezia could empathize. Headaches were an occupational hazard for firefighters. Hardly in the category of burns, broken bones or the inhalation of toxic fumes, but still a part of the physical toll exacted by the job. She had a medicine cabinet full of analgesics.

She scrutinized Mitch for another moment or two, eventually deciding that he was telling the truth about his condition. Pushing the matter to the back of her mind, she turned and poured herself some coffee.

"Noticed you and Fridge Randall seemed to be gettin' pretty friendly last night," J.T. commented after a couple of seconds, his tone a little sly.

Keezia's heart skipped a beat, but she managed to keep her expression under control and her hands steady. She'd reported to work braced for the possibility that one or more of her co-workers had seen her dancing—maybe even walking out of the door—with Fridge. Her MARTA commute had given her plenty of time to plan how she'd react if anyone raised the subject. She wouldn't deny anything. But she damned well wouldn't give away any information, either.

"Did you?" she returned, carefully spooning some sugar into her coffee.

"Uh-huh." J.T. clicked his tongue, obviously angling for information. Keezia gave him a bland-as-butter look, refusing to bite. After several moments of silence, he added a bit more bait. "You looked real fine, dancin' to that Luther Vandross tune."

"Which is somethin' nobody's ever gonna say about you, bro," Bobby Robbins jibed, ambling into the kitchen with a basketball under his arm. "I don't know where you were when God was handin' out rhythm, J.T., but it definitely wasn't in line."

Mitch snickered. Keezia managed to keep a straight face for a few seconds, then started to laugh. She supposed that some people might consider Bobby's comment offensive. She didn't. She'd seen J.T. Wilson attempt to dance on a number of occasions and pitiful was the only way to describe what she'd witnessed. The man had guts to spare when it came to fighting fires, but couldn't tell a downbeat from a downdraft to save his life.

"Yeah, yeah, yeah," J.T. said, aiming a hand gesture at his crew-cut colleague that definitely wasn't the Boy Scout salute.

"Those Arthur Murray ballroom lessons your fiancée signed you up for aren't working, John Thomas?" Keezia teased, figuring she owed him a jab or two for his nosiness about her and Fridge.

"Not that you'd notice," Bobby preemptively replied, bouncing the basketball against the kitchen's scarred linoleum floor. "Old J.T. made quite a spectacle of himself after you and Fridge faded from the scene last night, Keez. If you'd seem him trying to get down with that foxy—"

"Keezia went home with Fridge Randall?" Mitch interrupted, setting his coffee mug down with a clunk. He turned to his right, a combination of curiosity and astonishment vivid on his freckle-dusted face. "Jeez, Keezia. When did that happen?"

All the clever responses Keezia had rehearsed flew right out of her head. In their place came a replay of several of the more erotic images she'd conjured up after Fridge had called a halt to their kiss.

"My God, Fridge," she heard herself asking as her pulse scrambled and blood began to simmer. *"Exactly how long do you figure we'd need?"*

"I'm not figurin' 'exactlys' at this point, Keezia," came Fridge's provocative reply. *"What I do figure is that we have a lot of things to find out about each other and we shouldn't rush the job."*

"Uh—well—" she floundered, hoping her cheeks didn't look as warm as they felt.

"Hey, Carew!" someone in another section of the firehouse suddenly yelled. "You've got a call! Didn't give a name, but he sounds a hell of a lot like Fridge Randall!"

"Hello?"

"Hey, sugar."

Keezia caught her breath, her stomach fluttering. He shouldn't have called, she told herself firmly. Not here. Not now. But since he had...

Oh, Lord, was she glad of it!

"Fridge," she responded, keeping her voice low. The phone she'd been summoned to was in the station's main equipment room. Several of her co-workers were within earshot. She figured J.T., Mitch and/or Bobby would be showing up to satisfy their curiosity within the next minute or so, too.

"Been thinkin' about me?"

"Mmm..." She paused, pretending she needed to search her memory. Coy wasn't her usual style, but something about this question triggered the impulse to flirt. "You may have crossed my mind once or twice."

Fridge chuckled, his ego clearly unbruised by her feigned indifference. Had she been keeping score, Keezia would have given him a few extra points for his reaction. A lot of men perceived themselves as the center of the universe and expected every woman in their orbit to respond accordingly.

"Busy morning, huh?"

Someone on the other side of the room dropped something.

She started at the sound of metal clanging against concrete, her free hand lifting to the base of her throat. The artery there pulsed against her fingertips like a Mexican jumping bean.

"Keezia?"

"I'm here," she said quickly, willing herself to calm down. "And since you asked—no. It's been slow. Not a single call."

"It was pretty quiet the day before yesterday, too," Fridge observed. "The big excitement on the A shift was a single alarm involvin' a flaming Dumpster. Couple of winos got real ticked off when we knocked it down. I think they were plannin' a weenie roast."

Keezia laughed, imagining the scene. Then, growing serious, she declared, "I'm not saying I *want* there to be fires, you understand. People's houses burning down, businesses going up in smoke—if I could put an end to it, I would."

"Amen to that," the man on the other end of line interpolated with quiet fervor.

"But since I can't," she went on, repressing a sigh. "I'd like to feel like I'm doing something useful. You know what I mean, Fridge. Sitting around the station gets real old, real fast."

"I hear you, baby."

There was a pause. Keezia fiddled with the phone cord, acutely conscious of the thud-thud-thudding of her heart. The urge to flirt had evaporated. Which was just as well, all things considered. She'd never been very good at it.

"So," she finally said.

"So," Fridge responded, his voice slipping into a more intimate register. "Aren't you goin' to ask if I've been thinkin' about you?"

Keezia moistened her lips. "H-have you?"

"Uh-huh. I've been thinkin' how much I'd like to take you to dinner the day after tomorrow."

Four

Ralph Booker Randall took Keezia Lorraine Carew to dinner four times during the six weeks that followed. She reciprocated with a picnic lunch for a rafting trip down the Chattahoochee River and a pair of tickets to a concert by a jazz quartet she knew he greatly admired.

They had some very good times together. They laughed a great deal. They talked with increasing openness about who they thought they were and what they believed they wanted out of life. They listened to each other intently, too. But while they touched with escalating fervor and frequency, there was no rush to consummation.

As Fridge had said, they had a lot of things to find out about each other...

It was the fourth Monday in June and Keezia and Fridge were seated in a comparatively quiet corner of Atlanta's Varsity Restaurant. They'd decided to stop in for a snack after the Braves baseball game they'd been attending had been called in the bottom of the fifth because of rain. The timing of the decision had been unfortunate for the home team. Had it come an inning earlier, the Braves could have run into the locker room two runs up instead of four behind.

The Varsity was a sprawling establishment located near Georgia Tech. It specialized in hamburgers, chili dogs and a variety of deep-fried foodstuffs. It was a city institution, attracting local folks from all walks of life. Visiting celebrities—movie stars, musicians, champion athletes and big-name politicians—patronized it, too. Fridge had introduced Keezia to the place shortly after they'd met. She'd become a fan before she'd finished her second onion ring.

"Let me make sure I've got this straight," Keezia said after she'd finished washing down a gloriously greasy bite of onion ring with an inelegant slurp from her orange freeze. "Jackson met this woman on a fire call?"

"Uh-huh," Fridge affirmed, wiping his blunt-tipped fingers on a paper napkin. "Assumin' that you think catchin' someone as she keels over on you constitutes a meetin'."

"She actually fainted into his arms." She wasn't faulting the woman's melodramatic-sounding reaction; she simply wanted to make certain she had the facts right.

"Swooned like a Southern belle."

Keezia felt her lips twist. "Only she's from Boston."

"So I understand."

"And now she's taking up residence with Jackson and Lauralee."

"Jackson's house is a two-family place, sugar." The reminder was accompanied by a wry grin. "She's rentin' half of it. She'll be movin' in at the end of the week."

Keezia picked up another onion ring and munched on it, reviewing the remarkable story that Fridge had spent the past few minutes relating to her. It seemed that he, Jackson Miller and the other members of their station's A-shift crew had been summoned to a fire at a three-story apartment building about a week and a half ago. Theirs had been the second alarm call, and the blaze had been well involved by the time they'd arrived on the scene. Although they'd attacked the fire aggressively—masks on, ladders up, lines stretched into the building and nozzles blasting straight into the face of the flames— they'd lost the fight. While no one had been injured, the structure had been gutted.

Fridge and Jackson had been surveying the smoldering wreckage when an overwrought redhead had materialized behind them. Her distress at what she was seeing had been such that they'd both immediately assumed the worst—namely, that there was a body somewhere in the burned-out building.

Some quick questioning had alleviated this terrible fear. According to Fridge, he'd decided to back off at this point, figuring that Jackson might have better luck soothing the stressed-out woman if he wasn't looming within her line of sight. The next thing he'd known, the redhead was passed out cold and Jackson was cradling her against his chest like some romance-novel hero.

"Poleaxed" was the adjective Fridge had used to describe the expression his friend had been wearing.

"I don't know, Fridge," Keezia remarked, stirring the citrus-flavored slush of her orange freeze with a straw as she meditated on the situation. "The whole thing seems a little peculiar to me. This woman—uh, what did you say her name was again?"

"Phoebe." Fridge rattled the ice in his jumbo-sized soda cup then took a drink. "Phoebe Donovan."

"Right." She repeated the name silently, impressing it on her memory. Then she resumed. "This woman, Phoebe Donovan, goes out hunting for a new place to live after her apartment gets incinerated. And of all the possible things that could happen, she winds up with *Jackson Miller* as her new landlord. Jackson Miller, who's not just one of the firefighters who caught the call when her old building was burning down. Oh, no. He's also the very firefighter who kept her from nose-diving into the dirt when she passed out on the scene!" She shook her head. "Like I said. It seems…*peculiar.*"

"The Lord moves in mysterious ways, Keezia Lorraine."

Although this assertion was punctuated by a husky chuckle, Keezia knew that the faith from which it flowed was rock-solid serious. She recalled Fridge's description of Jackson's reaction to Phoebe Donovan's faint. He'd definitely implied that there'd been something out of the ordinary about the way his friend had behaved.

"You think there's some kind of plan at work here?" she asked, eyeing her companion curiously. She was uncertain how she felt about the possibility she'd just posited. That there was something appealing about the notion of a man and a woman being fated for each other was undeniable. Despite all she'd been through, she was still a sucker for the concept that some romantic relationships were meant to be. But having once been stuck like a bug in a spider web of emotion she hadn't consciously spun, she was unnerved by the idea of predestination. She'd worked hard to take control of her life since she'd walked out on Tyrell. If it turned out that there was an outside force pressing her buttons and pulling her strings...

"There's always a plan," Fridge declared. His dark gaze slid slowly from her eyes to her mouth. It lingered on her lips for what seemed like a very long time before returning to its starting point. Keezia's pulse was thoroughly snarled by the time it did. "The problem is figurin' out what it is and whether you want to go along with it."

There was a pause. After several heady seconds, Keezia glanced away. Her breathing pattern was shallow and uneven. She crossed her legs, right over left, and shifted in her chair. She shifted her position again a moment later. Then she re-crossed her legs, left over right. She knew her companion was tracking every movement. She could feel it with every fiber of her body.

Taking a steadying breath, Keezia returned her gaze to Fridge. He was leaning back in his chair, sipping at his soft drink. His posture was relaxed, even lazy. The expression in his eyes was anything but.

"Is she good-looking?" she asked.

"Who?"

"Phoebe Donovan."

"She's on the thin side." Fridge shrugged, the rippling play of his muscles obvious beneath the stretchy cotton of the Braves T-shirt he was wearing. "*Very* white."

"And she's some sort of medical doctor?"

"According to Jackson, she's a psychiatrist."

"Mmm."

"I told him havin' a shrink in the house might come in handy, considerin' the problems he's havin' with Lauralee."

Keezia froze in the act of picking up another onion ring. She remembered the hint of father-daughter discord she'd picked up on at the retirement party the night she and Fridge had kissed—really kissed—for the first time.

"Problems?" she echoed, genuinely concerned. "What kind of problems?"

"Puberty, basically."

"*Huh?*"

Fridge grinned. "Jackson's been havin' a tough time adjustin' to bein' the daddy of a teenage daughter. The notion that Lauralee's goin' to be gettin' her driver's permit next year has him wakin' up in the middle of the night in a cold sweat. And then there's the fact that she's already got a couple of boys—"

"Hey, Ms. Carew!"

Keezia started at the unexpected greeting then turned in her seat.

"Hey, girl," she said to the plump young woman who'd come bopping up behind her. She glanced back at Fridge. "Fridge, this is Vanessa Temple. I met her through that mentoring program your mama helped set up at the community center. Vanessa, this is Ralph Randall, Miz Helen Rose's son. He's with the fire department, too."

"Vanessa," Fridge said, nodding.

"Hey," the girl responded, scrutinizing him with undisguised interest. After a few moments she shifted her assessing gaze to Keezia.

"How's it going?" Keezia asked, ignoring the teenager's speculative expression.

"Okay." Vanessa patted at her bleached, slickly styled hair. Her eyes darted toward Fridge, then back to Keezia once again. "I put my papers in for that apprentice program you told me about."

"You did?" Keezia was pleased. And, frankly, a little surprised. She'd told Vanessa about a lot of opportunities. This was the first time the girl had followed up on one.

"Uh-huh. I'm s'posed to go on an interview next week."

"That's terrific."

"I guess." Vanessa grimaced and scratched her nose. It was a delicate maneuver, considering the thin gold ring in her left nostril. "There's about a zillion other girls applyin', though, so the competition's really intense."

"What about your—"

"Oh!" the teenager interrupted, staring over Keezia's shoulder. "There's Derek." She waved vigorously. *"Derek!"*

The young man she was hailing was buck-toothed, bespectacled and build like a black soda straw. Keezia's first thought was that his attenuated physique probably made him the target of a lot of razzing—like, "He's so skinny, he could use a Froot Loop for a hula hoop!" Her second was that he was a definite improvement over the sullen-eyed punk Vanessa had been keeping company with earlier in the year. Better a geek than a gangbanger.

"Derek, this is Keezia Carew," Vanessa said, taking his hand in a proprietary manner. "Remember, I told you about her? From the center? She's the firefighter? Ms. Carew, this is Derek. Derek White."

"Hey, ma'am," the young man said, dipping his head slightly and flashing a shy smile.

"Nice to meet you, Derek," Keezia replied. She gestured at Fridge. "This is my friend, Ralph Randall."

"He's with the fire department, too," Vanessa supplemented. "And he's Miz Helen Rose Randall's son."

"Derek," Fridge said gravely, extending his hand.

"Mr. Randall," the young man answered, taking the proffered appendage and shaking it. He squared his shoulders and drew himself up as he did so. For a moment, Keezia thought the storklike movement was male posturing—a testosterone-induced effort to demonstrate that he wasn't intimidated by

Fridge's size and obviously superior strength. Then she realized that it signified something much more positive. Fridge was treating Derek White with respect and he was responding accordingly.

She recalled observing a similar pattern in Fridge's dealings with several of the young men at their church. There was something in his manner that made them want to stand tall in his eyes. Earning Ralph Booker Randall's good opinion seemed to matter to them.

"Derek's goin' to Georgia State next year," Vanessa announced.

"Congratulations," Keezia said, meaning it.

"That's somethin' to be proud of," Fridge concurred. "I went to Tech myself, but GSU's a fine school."

"He's got a scholarship."

"Vanessa, honey, you don't have to be tellin' everybody that," Derek muttered, plainly embarrassed.

"I know I don't *have* to," Vanessa answered, snuggling close and giggling. "I do it because I *want* to."

"Better to have her braggin' on you in public than raggin' on you in private, Derek," Fridge advised with a chuckle.

Keezia felt the dynamics of the conversation shift. All of a sudden, it was the brothers against the sisters. Derek's previous awkwardness evaporated.

"Oh, she does that, too," he said, giving Fridge an I-know-you-understand-where-I'm-coming-from grin.

Keezia resisted the urge to roll her eyes. *Men!* There were moments when even the best of them made her wonder why the good Lord hadn't gone back to the drawing board after he'd examined his first human creation.

Vanessa took a swat at her companion. "I do not, Derek White!"

"Sure you do, girl." Derek was on a roll now. "What about that number you did on me in the car the other night on the way back from Woodrow's birthday party?"

Vanessa slammed her fists on her not inconsiderable hips and glared. "I was s'posed to keep quiet after you humiliated me by droolin' all over that bitch Josey Jackson?"

Derek opened and shut his mouth several times, clearly unprepared for this frontal attack. Finally he rallied and said,
"Well, I wouldn't have noticed her if you hadn't been makin'
eyes at Luther Kincaid!"

Vanessa gave Keezia the female equivalent of the I-know-
you-understand-where-I'm-coming-from look Derek had given
Fridge a few moments earlier. "Excuse us, please," she requested, biting off the words. Then she glommed onto Derek's
arm and more or less dragged him away.

"Young love," Fridge wryly editorialized when the couple
was out of earshot.

"Young *something*," Keezia retorted, trying not to think of
herself at Vanessa's age. "And you didn't help much with
that comment about her ragging on him in private."

"I wouldn't have said it if I'd realized I was touchin' on a
sore subject."

"Have you ever known a relationship where it wasn't?"
She expelled a huffy little breath. "Just because you men can't
take a little constructive criticism—"

"What you women call 'a little constructive criticism' is
usually pickin' a man apart, then tryin' to stitch him back
together after rearrangin' the pieces!"

"Oh, you think so?"

"Yes, I think so!"

"Well—" Keezia's mind blanked. It suddenly dawned on
her that she and Fridge were having their first real argument.
It also occurred to her that the topic involved was borderline
ridiculous.

"Well, *what?*" came the irritated prompt.

A giggle tickled its way up Keezia's throat. "G-give me a
second," she asked, fighting to keep a straight face. "I'll come
up with s-something."

Fridge narrowed his eyes. Then he, too, apparently recognized the absurdity of what was going on. His lips started to
twitch. A moment later, they were both laughing.

"I can't believe I actually let the words 'you women' come
out of my mouth," he eventually said, shaking his head.

"I got in a 'you men' first," Keezia reminded him.

"I think you had good reason."

"Well..." She cocked her head and gave him a little smile. "Maybe."

There was a brief pause. Then Fridge asked, "So, Vanessa Temple's one of your counselees down at the community center?"

"Uh-huh."

"Mama says you have a real knack for gettin' girls to listen to you."

"I try," Keezia said, warmed by the secondhand compliment. Then her innate honestly compelled her to add a caveat. "But getting somebody like Vanessa to listen isn't the same as getting her to *hear*."

"Now isn't that the truth." Fridge's expression suggested that he was reflecting on some of his more challenging experiences as a youth counselor.

"Still—" she toyed with a now cold onion ring, then pushed the paper plate on which it was aside "—I feel good about working with the mentoring program. And I'm glad your mama thinks I'm doing something right with it. I know I disappointed her when I decided I couldn't deal with the situation at the women's shelter anymore. I wish I could have found some way to explain why I quit."

Fridge reached over and covered her hand. Keezia trembled at the tenderness of his touch. "You didn't have to. She understood."

"You really think so?"

"I know so, sugar."

Keezia worried her lower lip with the edge of her teeth for a moment, then eased her gaze away from his. Taking a deep breath, she tried to articulate a truth she'd never fully acknowledged to anyone, including herself.

"It's not that I didn't believe in what was going on there," she said slowly. "At the shelter, I mean. I did. I *do*. It's just that I'd look at the women coming in—faces bruised, bones broken, too scared to spit—and I kept seeing myself. And then they'd start talking about the men who beat them up and every word out of their mouths was something *I'd* said about me and Tyrell."

She paused, then forced herself to meet Fridge's eyes again. He sustained her gaze steadily, but made no effort to speak. *It's up to you,* his expression said. *However much—however little—you want to tell.*

Keezia took another deep breath and forged on. "There were times I almost hated them for making me remember. And I know some of them picked up on the way I felt. *That's* the real reason I had to quit, Fridge. Because I was adding to their hurt. I mean, they came in asking for help. But instead of holding out my hand as a friend, I looked down my nose at them like they were dirt!"

Fridge's fingers tightened around hers. He shook his head. "I don't believe that for a second."

Her pulse fluttered at the intensity of his confidence in her. Still she said, "It's true."

"No."

"You think you know what I do—how I am—better than I do?"

"Maybe." Fridge relaxed his grip, then released her hand completely. "Sometimes. Yes, I do."

The withdrawal of physical contact provoked an odd combination of emotions in Keezia. Somewhere in the welter of them came the compulsion to open a subject she had a great many reasons to want to keep sealed.

"That night I finally told you about me and Tyrell—" she began.

"I didn't handle that very well, baby," Fridge cut in, his voice low and tight. There was a pain in his eyes. And something even more difficult for her to look at. It was shame. "I got *angry.*"

Keezia blinked, shaken by his reaction. She hadn't been about to chastise him for what had happened that night. Quite the contrary.

"You got angry *for* me, Fridge," she countered softly. "Not *at* me. I admit it took me a while to understand the difference, but I understand it now. And even when I didn't..."

"What?"

She looked him squarely in the face, wondering why she hadn't said what she was about to say before. She'd owed this good man a debt of gratitude for a long, long time. It was time to acknowledge it and pay up.

"Do you know, you're just about the only person in the world who's never acted like it was my fault?" she finally asked.

Fridge furrowed his forehead. "You mean...Tyrell's abusing you?"

She nodded.

"How the *hell* could anybody think that was your fault?"

His use of the swear word was revealing. The fact that he didn't immediately apologize for it, even more so. Keezia had only heard Fridge curse twice before. He'd begged her pardon on both occasions.

"Oh, Fridge." The man sitting across from her wasn't naive in any way, shape or form. But there were times when his bred-in-the-bone sense of decency created blind spots about human nature. "Ask any woman who's ever been beaten up by her husband or boyfriend. She'll tell you the blame almost always gets turned around on her. It's in the questions people ask, even when they're trying to be sympathetic. Questions like, 'What did you say to make him hit you?' Or, 'What didn't you do that you should have done so he wouldn't get mad?' Or, 'If he's so bad...why do you stay with him?'"

Fridge seemed stunned. "I never realized..."

"I know."

There was another pause. Keezia glanced in the direction Vanessa had taken Derek. She spotted the young couple on the other side of the room. Their arms were pretzeled around each other's bodies. Their lips were mashed together in a soulful kiss.

Young love, indeed, she thought, then added a brief prayer that this adolescent passion wouldn't have any lasting consequences. There were too many babies having babies as it was without sixteen-year-old Vanessa Temple joining the list.

She felt Fridge reclaim her hand and turned back to face him. Something in his expression told her that he'd seen what she'd seen and had had a very similar reaction to it. She remembered a fragment of a conversation she'd once overheard him having with a pair of teenage boys. Something about the true test of a man not being his ability to make a child, but to take care of it.

Fridge stroked her knuckles gently with the pad of his thumb, holding her gaze. Eventually he asked, "You want children, Keezia Lorraine?"

Her heart skipped a beat. Maybe two. The image of a solidly built little boy scampered across her mind's eye. The child was dark-skinned, with coffee-bean brown eyes and a broad, well-defined nose. He threw himself, laughing, into the waiting, well-muscled arms of the strong black man who was his father.

Keezia blinked away the image. The urge to avert her gaze was very strong but she resisted it. Looking directly at Fridge, she answered his question with what she knew to be the truth.

"Yes, I want children," she said. "But I want some other things first."

Fridge was still pondering this response when he escorted Keezia to her car about fifteen minutes later. He hadn't followed up on the answer for a variety of reasons. His inquiry about whether she wanted children hadn't been planned. It had just slipped out. Which wasn't to say that he hadn't thought about Keezia having kids—*his* kids—on a number of occasions. He very definitely had. But to push that issue when there were so many others to be pursued and resolved...

It would have been premature, to say the least.

With this realization firmly in mind, he'd been pleased to let their discussion drift off the topic of procreation and into much more casual territory. Except that "drift" wasn't really the right word to describe how their conversation had evolved. He'd done a fair amount of verbal steering. Keezia had stuck

her oar in, too—so to speak. It had been her decision to bring
the evening to a close by glancing at her wristwatch and stat-
ing that it was time for her to be heading home.

They'd both made quick stops in the Varsity's rest rooms
before heading out into the June night. The torrential down-
pour that had halted the Braves' game had given way to a fine
mist. Had Fridge been alone, he wouldn't have bothered opening his umbrella. But Keezia's presence made it impossible
for him to keep it closed. There was no way Helen Rose Randall's son could allow a lady to get wet when he had the
equipment on hand to keep her dry.

"How's the car runnin'?" he asked as they reached the
driver's side of Keezia's vehicle.

Keezia turned and looked up at him, the illumination from
the parking lot's lights adding a hint of ethereal delicacy to
her exotic features. "Better than ever."

"'Ever' being defined as?"

"Well..."

"Uh-huh. I thought so."

"It hasn't quit once since I got it back from Jamal," she
pointed out. "He did a good job."

"I told you he would."

"*And* he charged me a fair price."

"I told you that as well, as I recall."

"Tried to, anyway," Keezia corrected, arching her brows.
"As I recall, I didn't much want to listen."

Fridge caught a whiff of her musk-spice scent. He swallowed hard, shifting his weight from one foot to the other.
"You were just lookin' out for your interests."

"No." His companion shook her head. The movement emphasized the fluid loveliness of her throat. His gaze started to
slide down the line of that long, smooth throat. He hauled it
back up. "I think *you* were the one doing that. I was acting
like an—"

"Independent woman?" he swiftly inserted. He understood
that she was trying to apologize and he appreciated the thought
but it really wasn't necessary. Besides, he didn't want her
getting down on herself. She was too fine a woman for that.

Keezia cocked her head, obviously a bit puzzled by his mood. "Something like that."

"Nothing wrong with independence in a woman, sugar."

"Oh?"

"Uh-huh. I'm all for it." He waited a beat then added, "Up to a point."

For a second or two, it appeared that Keezia was taking his statement seriously. Then, suddenly, she started to smile. The oh-*now*-I-know-what-you're-up-to curving of her lush lips caused a fair amount of Fridge's blood to divert from his brain and rush southward.

"And exactly what point might that be, Brother Randall?" she inquired, her voice like molten honey. She lifted her chin as she spoke, her eyes shimmering with a uniquely feminine form of provocation.

"Well..." Fridge let the word trail off, pretending to consider. His body was thrumming with anticipation. He was intensely grateful for the slight give in the fit of the jeans he had on. "If you were to *independently* put your arms around my neck—"

"Like this?"

"Uh-huh."

"Not too independent for you?"

"Unh-uh."

"And what if I were to...independently...move a little closer?"

The tips of her fabric-covered breasts brushed against the front of his T-shirted chest. She followed this up with a subtle swivel of her hips that made his breath wedge at the top of his throat. He slipped his free hand around her waist, fingers splaying in the small of her back. He wasn't sure whether he was trying to hold her still or draw her even nearer.

"Are we beyond the point yet?" Keezia asked in a dulcetly dangerous voice.

Fridge blinked, his sensation-hazed brain refusing to provide a context for her question. "What point is that, baby?"

She was relishing his confusion. He could see it. Feel it. It gave her a kick, testing her feminine power on him. It gave him a kick, too. Because if she'd reached the stage where she was able to take the seductive lead and consciously exercise her womanly wiles, it meant that she was finally purging off the psychological poisons she'd been force-fed during her marriage to Tyrell Babcock.

"The point where there stops being nothing wrong with a woman's independence."

"Oh." Fridge shifted his hand an inch or so. He felt Keezia quiver. He experienced a flash of possessiveness. The strength of it surprised him. "We're nowhere close."

"You're...sure?"

"Mmm." He massaged, very gently. He didn't want to take this woman, he reminded himself. He didn't want to own her. He wanted her to share herself with him. He wanted her to *give*...and receive in return.

"So there wouldn't be anything wrong with me sort of easing your head down..."

Oh.

"...and sort of bringing myself up..."

Oh, yes.

"...and then..."

Oh, yes. *Please.*

Their mouths met. Mated.

They both moaned.

Keezia's lips opened. Fridge delved into the moist warmth behind her teeth, his tongue twining with hers in a slow, evocative dance. The taste of peppermint told him that he was not the only one who'd resorted to a breath freshener while in the bathroom. The realization that she'd readied herself for this kiss was intensely pleasurable to him.

She tilted her head one way. He tilted his the other. The kiss deepened. Grew more demanding. The slow, evocative dance became blatantly sexual.

"Mmm..." Keezia breathed when they finally eased apart. She ran her pretty pink tongue over her full bottom lip as though licking up his flavor. The muscles of Fridge's belly clenched in a very primitive reaction. The give in his jeans ran out and the denim garment started to bind.

"Keezia," he whispered.

She lifted her hand and stroked her fingertips along his mustache much the way she'd done six weeks before in the foyer of her apartment. Then she traced the shape of his lips with delicate precision. His tongue darted out of its own accord, flicking across her flesh.

"At the risk of pushing my womanly independence too far," she murmured, her eyes sultry as the summer soon to come. "I want to say that you are one fine kisser, Ralph Booker Randall."

A laugh rumbled up from deep within his chest. Where he found the air for it, Fridge didn't know. He figured it had been at least a couple minutes since he'd been able to draw a breath.

"I can do *much* better, sugar," he eventually managed to assure her.

But not in the parking lot of the Varsity.

And not with a stand-on-her-own female firefighter who had a 7:00 a.m. roll call to answer.

The phone started ringing as soon as Keezia walked into her apartment. She nearly tripped over Shabazz as she dashed to answer it. While this was partly her cat's fault for doing absolutely nothing to get out of the way, she knew the primary blame for the near-collision rested with her. Kissing Fridge had left her feeling dizzy and drunk. She could barely walk a straight line.

"Hello?" she said into the mouthpiece.

"Hey, Keezia."

Her semisolid knees liquefied. She sagged against the wall, her body temperature soaring by several degrees. Shabazz yowled and batted a stuffed mouse at her foot.

"Checking up on me, Fridge?" she asked after a moment, shoving the pet toy aside with the toe of her shoe.

"I wouldn't dare."

"Then why did you call?"

"Aside from the fact that I wanted to tell you what a good time I had tonight, you mean?"

"Mmm." Keezia struggled to keep the smile that was

spreading across her face from revealing itself in her voice. No need to let the man on the other end of the line get too cocky.

Shabazz *meeee-rowed* again, making circle eights around her ankles.

"Well," Fridge replied. "I was wonderin' how an independent woman such as yourself might react to the idea of our gettin' together the day after tomorrow instead of the day after that."

Keezia blinked. "Are you talking about...Wednesday?"

"Uh-huh."

"But aren't you scheduled to work then?"

"Not anymore. There was a message on my machine when I got home tellin' me I've got a temporary reassignment. A station on the south side. Some kind of emergency personnel problem."

Keezia fiddled with the phone cord, her fingers only marginally more steady than her pulse. "So...you're going to be pulling the C shift?"

"Uh-huh."

"Same as me."

"Seems that way."

"No double duty?"

"Nope. I'm off the A for at least a month."

"You don't say."

"Oh, but I do."

"And you want us to get together Wednesday instead of Thursday."

There was a long pause. Then, very deliberately, "It doesn't necessarily have to be instead of, sugar."

"I see." She did, too. And the implications of what she saw...

"I was thinking maybe you could come over to my place and I could make you some of my daddy's famous ribs."

She managed a little laugh. "You've been promising to do that."

"And I'm a man who makes a point of keepin' his promises."

The words were spoken lightly, but Keezia knew that they'd come from the heart.

You can trust him, something deep inside her whispered. It was the same something that had whispered to her six weeks earlier.

I know, she responded silently. *I know...and I do.*

"Keezia?"

She straightened. The sensual intoxication she'd experienced a few minutes before had given way to a clear-eyed sense of exhilaration. She was no longer light-headed. But for the first time in a long, long time, she felt light of heart.

"Can I bring dessert?" she asked.

A rich chuckle came down the line. The sound of it tickled inside her ear like a feather, triggering a delicious tingle of anticipation. She lifted a hand to her breasts. Her nipples were taut beneath her clothing. Her heart was beating very quickly.

"You can bring anything you want, Keezia Lorraine."

Five

B-b-rring!

Fridge awoke with a start, his transition from deep sleep to full awareness almost instantaneous. His mind immediately seized on two facts.

The first was that he was at home in his own bed rather than on a cot at the fire station.

The second was that he'd been dreaming.

Vividly.

Voluptuously.

With very obvious physiological consequences.

B-b-rring.

He reached to his left and picked up the bedside phone. The digital readout on the clock next to the phone informed him that it was 10:58 a.m.

"H'llo?" he said into the receiver, telling himself not to get his hopes up.

No answer.

He cleared his throat and tried again. "Hello?"

"Ralph?"

The hopes he wasn't supposed to get up crashed like the stock market of 1929. A certain part of his anatomy went into a bit of a decline, too.

"Good mornin', Mama," he responded, sitting up. Bedsheets slid down his torso, puddling around his hips. He scratched his chest.

"Ralph Booker Randall, what are you doing home?"

Fridge reminded himself with a trace of asperity that he was a grown man. He was well beyond the stage where he could be intimidated by the sound of his mama's distinctive contralto voice invoking his full name like an angel on Judgment Day.

Whether he was beyond the stage of being intimidated if that invocation was accompanied by one of Helen Rose Randall's uniquely penetrating stares was open to debate. Fortunately, this was not a face-to-face conversation.

"Aside from talkin' to you?" he inquired, smothering a yawn. Now that his brain knew he wasn't going to be rushing off to fight a fire, his body was shifting out of its peak response mode.

"Aren't you supposed to be at work?"

Wasn't he supposed to be—?

Oh, Lord. Of course!

"I worked yesterday, Mama," he quickly explained, mentally chiding himself for not having alerted to her to the change in his schedule. While his mother had always been prone to poking her nose into his business, her need to keep tabs on him had escalated since his father had succumbed to cancer, four years ago. Exasperating though he sometimes found the effort, Fridge did his best to keep her informed. He knew the depth and darkness of the void that Willie Leroy Randall's death had left in her life.

"How's that?" Willie Leroy's widow asked sharply.

"Temporary reassignment. I'm on the C shift for a month instead of the A."

"Oh." There was a pause. Then, "I guess that's why you weren't there when I called yesterday."

Fridge swallowed another yawn, remembering with a mix of amusement and irritation the trio of hang-ups that he'd found on his answering machine when he'd arrived home shortly after 7:25 a.m. He'd suspected their source, now he was sure of it.

"Still can't bring yourself to leave a message, huh?" he teased. If truth be told, he wasn't particularly fond of answering machines either, but he still made use of them.

"Don't you have anything better to do than loll around in bed?"

Fridge's mind suddenly flashed back to the intensely sensual look he'd seen on Keezia's face in the parking lot of the Varsity. Desire licked at him as he remembered the yearning brilliance of her topaz eyes and the yielding ripeness of her lips.

He felt his body stir and restiffen. The fingers of his free hand clenched, tangling in the wrinkled bedsheets. *Dessert,* he thought. She'd asked him if she could bring—

The sound of his mother saying his name jerked Fridge out of his reverie. He shifted his position awkwardly, unnerved by his susceptibility.

"Is there somethin' I can do for you, Mama?" he asked, struggling to keep his voice even.

No answer.

"Mama?" he repeated.

"I called yesterday about tomorrow," came the rather cryptic response. "But since you're not working today, maybe tonight would be better."

"'Better'?" Fridge echoed, his well-developed filial alarm system going off. A girl, he thought grimly. She's gone out and found me a girl.

Again.

"Uh-huh. My friend, Ethel Delaney—you remember her, don't you? She worked with me on that literacy fund-raiser last year? Well, her niece Geneva is in town from Mobile and—"

"No, Mama." It was rude and Fridge knew it. He also knew that a fast, flat-out rejection was the only way to stop his mother when she had matchmaking on her mind. Tactful attempts to sidestep or finesse the issue didn't work. He'd tried such tactics enough times in the past to be stone-cold certain of that.

"What did you say?"

"I said, no."

"Well, why not?" Helen Rose Randall demanded, matching bluntness with bluntness. "Ethel Delaney says Geneva is a sweet girl—"

"I'm sure Miz Delaney does," Fridge interrupted flatly. "And I'm sure this Geneva is like honey in a comb. But the answer's still no. *N-O*, thank you very much, Mama, but no."

"What's so wrong with a mother wanting her only son to settle down with a nice girl and give her some grandbabies?"

The mention of children evoked a strong surge of emotion within Fridge. He wanted kids. He always had. But it wasn't until he'd met Keezia Carew that he'd known with whom he wanted to have them.

"You want children, Keezia Lorraine?" he'd asked her the night before last.

"Yes, I want children," she'd replied. *"But I want some other things first."*

God willing, she would get those other things.

God willing, at least a few of them would be from him.

"Ralph?"

Fridge tilted his head back. "There's nothin' wrong with it. And I'd like to oblige you. Believe me, I would."

"How can I believe that when you won't even meet Ethel Delaney's niece? I was thinking I could invite her over to supper tonight—"

"I've got a date tonight."

His mother said nothing for a good thirty seconds. Fridge wasn't alarmed by her protracted silence. He knew that she was thinking. He could practically hear her brain working. He braced himself.

"Since when?" she finally asked.

It was not the question he'd anticipated. He tested it for a trap, but found none. After a fractional pause he said, "Since about thirty-six hours ago."

His mother took a moment to calculate the implications of this response. "You made a date in the middle of the night?"

He gulped, feeling his maturity peel away. How did the woman do it? How did she reduce him to the status of an errant schoolboy simply by changing the inflection of her voice?

"Uh—"

"What kind of female would say yes to such a thing?"

"You tell me, Mama," he retorted, exasperated. "It's Keezia Carew."

Again, there was silence on the other end of the line. But this time Fridge couldn't hear his mother thinking. He was too busy accusing himself of being six kinds of fool for blurting out something he'd intended to keep quiet for a little while longer.

It wasn't that he was ashamed of what was—or wasn't— going on between him and Keezia. How could he be? He just felt very...protective...of their developing relationship. And as deeply as he loved his mother—

"Well, praise the Lord," Helen Rose Randall suddenly exclaimed, her voice vibrant with emotion. "It's about time you admitted to it."

"What?" Fridge sat bolt upright.

"I said, it's about time—"

"You knew I've been seein' Keezia?"

"Well, of course."

"You *knew*...and you didn't *say* anything?"

"What was I supposed to say?"

Considering her loquaciousness where some of his previous lady friends were concerned, Fridge found it difficult to believe that this was a serious question.

"How?" he asked after a moment.

"How did I manage to keep my mouth shut?"

"No!" Which wasn't to say he wasn't curious. He simply had a more pressing question to pursue. "How did you find out?"

"Oh. That." A small sniff. "Well, when a son who's always been good about keeping his loving mama apprised of his business suddenly stops talking to her about what's going on in his social life, she naturally gets a little curious.''

"It didn't occur to you—my 'lovin' mama—that there might be nothin' to tell?''

"I considered that possibility," his mother allowed. "But then I went to the beauty parlor late last month and my stylist mentioned that she'd spotted you cuddled up next to a *very* attractive young lady at some jazz concert.''

He almost groaned. "And you automatically assumed this very attractive young lady was Keezia.''

"Shame on you! I didn't *assume* anything. I asked for a description, then I *deduced* it was Keezia. Paulette—that's my stylist—has a fine eye for detail.''

"I'll just bet she has.''

"Naturally, I kept a watch out after that," his mother continued, apparently deciding to ignore his sardonic interpolation. "And when I saw the way the pair of you were looking at each other in church two weeks ago...''

Fridge exhaled heavily, visualizing the scene. He'd sung in the choir two Sundays ago. Keezia had been seated in the congregation about two-thirds of the way back, off to the right. Halfway through the first verse of his first solo, a shaft of light had come pouring in through one of the stained-glass windows, enveloping her in a lambently golden glow. She'd turned her face up in response to the illumination, like a flower lifting toward the sun. He'd never seen anything so alluringly lovely in his life. That his voice hadn't cracked in response to the surge of passion he'd felt was a minor miracle.

"Keezia and I have known each other for three years, Mama," he pointed out, wondering uneasily how obvious his interest had been. How many of his fellow churchgoers had realized that he was yearning after an earthly love when he was supposed to be wrapped up in the Holy Spirit? "We've looked at each other a lot of times.''

"Uh-huh.'' The response was dry. Implicit in it was the warning that if he actually thought she was buying a single syllable of his shuck-and-jive dance around the facts, he'd best think again. "And you probably make a regular practice of making out in the parking lot of the Varsity, too."

Fridge nearly choked. *How in the name of—*

Oh.

Of course.

It had to be.

"Vanessa Temple," he said through gritted teeth.

"She happened to be at the community center yesterday when I stopped by," his mother blithely confirmed. "A sweet child, although I don't know what possessed her to go putting that ugly little ring through her nose. I can't abide all this body piercing that's going on."

"Mama—" Fridge hesitated, torn between a need to know and a desire to avoid giving offense.

"What, honey?"

The need to know won out. "Have you talked to Keezia about any of this?"

"Of course not." The answer held a tinge of disappointment that he would ask such a thing. It was followed by a soft sigh. "I won't deny having some expectations that first day at church when I introduced the two of you. And I did a little nudging when I should have had the sense to hold back. But then I got to know Keezia better and...well, let's just say I realized that she has a lot of things to work through."

Fridge's heart swelled with unalloyed affection for the woman on the other end of the line. "She's needed time, Mama," he said simply. "Both of us have. And, much as I'd like to tell you otherwise...the workin' through isn't finished. Not for either of us."

"Your father waited five years before I was ready to say yes to him," Helen Rose Randall recalled with a wistfully nostalgic laugh.

"He told me more than a few times he would've waited twice that long and still counted himself very lucky."

"My Willie Leroy was a patient man."

"No argument with that."

"He was a good man, too. Just like his son."

Fridge was deeply touched. While he'd never doubted his

mother's love, the comparison she'd just made resonated within him like a very special blessing.

"Mama—" he began, his voice slightly roughened by emotion.

"You know," she interrupted, her tone turning brisk. "Rebecca Matthews—did you ever meet her? I can't recall. Maybe not. She and I went to Washington last fall to lobby Congress on that school-to-work training bill. Anyway, her youngest boy is single and I'll just bet he'd be a perfect match for Ethel Delaney's niece. Jerome, I believe his name is. He's some kind of manager out at Lenox Mall. I think I'll call Rebecca right this very minute and ask her whether she thinks he'd be interested in meeting Geneva."

Fridge didn't balk at the sudden redirection of their conversation. He knew he'd find another occasion to tell his mother what her words had meant to him. He might also get around to inquiring whether she'd orchestrated this entire phone call to goad him into 'fessing up about Keezia.

"You're goin' to give Jerome a choice?" he asked dryly.

"Everybody gets a choice, Ralph Booker." The response was as crisp as a cracker and utterly confident. "They may have to be shoved into realizing what it is, but they definitely get one."

"Uh-huh."

"I have to hang up now, honey. Give Keezia my best when you see her tonight, will you?"

He smiled a little, thinking ahead. "I'll definitely do that, Mama."

"Be sure to give her *your* best, too."

Whether his mother had intended her parting remark the way his Keezia-fixated brain immediately interpreted it was something Ralph Randall never built up sufficient nerve to ask. But the comment did prompt him to make certain that there was a fresh supply of condoms in the drawer of his night table.

It also inspired him to change the sheets on his king-sized bed.

* * *

"Sweet," Keezia said about seven hours later. She licked a smear of Fridge's version of his father's barbecue sauce off her right index finger, trying to discern the secrets of its distinctive flavor. She'd already figured out the obvious components. "It's definitely something…sweet."

"Sweet covers a lot of territory, sugar," her host replied, shooing a fly away from his face with a lazy wave of his hand.

It was nearing dusk. Keezia and Fridge were sitting on the back porch of his small, Grant Park home. Although the temperature had hovered near ninety for most of the day, a gentle breeze made the air feel cooler. It also carried the happy sounds of children playing tag, some distance away.

"Corn syrup," she said, deciding it couldn't be anything as obvious as brown sugar.

"Uh-uh."

"Molasses."

"Nope."

"Honey?" Keezia put a little spin on the word, hinting that it might be an endearment…as well as a crucial ingredient in Willie Leroy Randall's delicious barbecue sauce.

Fridge's mouth quirked, making it clear that he'd gotten the message. After a moment, he shook his head.

She was running out of ideas. Sweet…sweet…

"Peach juice!"

He laughed. The sound was rich and full and free.

Keezia nibbled her lower lip, watching as Fridge succumbed to amusement. She'd seldom seen him so loose. So bonelessly relaxed. Whereas she…

She wasn't tense, exactly, she told herself. More like keyed up. Extra alert. Unusually expectant. All her senses were abnormally acute this beautiful Wednesday evening.

Even her hearing was sharper than normal. How else to explain her ability to detect each time the lub-a-dub beat of her heart accelerated into a lub-a-dub-dub?

Now was one of those times. Now, as she let her gaze wander down Fridge's broad-shouldered, narrow-hipped, long-legged body. His dark skin gleamed like polished mahogany in the fading sunlight, its rich color in sensual contrast to the sleeveless runner's top and wash-faded jeans he had on.

"Give up?" Fridge asked, his voice several notes lower than it had been the last time he'd spoken.

She lifted her eyes to his, feeling herself flush. "How about a hint?"

He expelled a breath on a long, hissing sigh. Then he gave her a crooked smile. "It's something people drink."

"Iced tea."

"Uh-uh."

She tilted her head to one side, the gold hoop earrings she was wearing swinging gently. It couldn't be anything alcoholic, she mused. Fridge had told her that his father had taken a temperance pledge at age eighteen and stuck by it, faithfully, throughout his adult life.

After a few moments she ventured the name of a soft drink which, rumor had it, was nothing less than carbonated prune juice.

"Shame on you for thinkin' such a thing," Fridge chided. "My daddy was born and raised in Atlanta. The secret of his sauce was—*is*—strictly local."

Atlanta.

Strictly local.

Could it—

"Are you saying you used *Coca-Cola* on those ribs?"

Fridge spread his hands in affirmation.

"I never would have guessed," she said frankly.

"Not many people do. I added a pinch of cayenne, too."

"And what's the secret of your potato salad?" She tried to think of something quintessentially southern. "Grits?"

"Come here." A gesture. "I'll whisper it."

Keezia waited a beat or two, wanting to make it crystal clear that she wasn't in the habit of responding when a man quirked his finger at her. Then she shifted her position and settled herself thigh to thigh with Fridge.

He leaned in and cupped his hand around her ear.

She let her eyelids flutter closed.

He whispered two syllables, his warm breath fanning her skin.

"Mmm..." Keezia sighed, savoring their closeness.

And then she registered what had been said.

"Store-bought?" she repeated, her eyelids popping open. She stared at him with feigned indignation. "You actually fed me *store-bought* potato salad?"

"'Fraid so, sugar." Fridge flashed a roguishly unapologetic grin. "Potato salad doesn't hold much of a challenge for me. What can I say? I'm the kind of man who needs a sense of *danger* when it comes to food preparation."

Keezia snorted. "Excuse me?"

"It's a carryover from the times when men were hunters," he informed her earnestly. "When it was eat or get eaten. When the diners could become the dinner if they didn't watch their step."

"When potential entrées had teeth." She couldn't believe she was going along with this.

"Exactly."

"And because of this, you need something that gives you an—uh—adrenaline rush before you can really get down and get cooking."

"Uh-huh." Fridge's eyes glinted.

"Like a flaming barbecue pit."

"Or some of those big, sharp cleavers."

Keezia began to laugh. She couldn't help it. And as she laughed, she leaned into Fridge, resting her head against his chest. She felt his left arm slide around her waist. She nestled closer.

Her laughter faded to a breathy chuckle then trailed off into a long, soft sigh. He felt so-o-o-o-o good.

"You don't seem to be givin' my gender-based theory of food preparation patterns the respect it deserves, Sister Carew," Fridge murmured after a few moments, brushing his lips against her tightly curled hair.

She eased back an inch or two, angling her head so she could look up into his face. "You've actually had women *believe* that caveman rap of yours?"

To say that this was not the best time to bring up the subject of other women was a little like suggesting that a skunk might be a less than welcome guest at a formal garden party. Had Keezia been able to recall the flippant question, she would have. But she couldn't, so she had to let it hang there and watch her companion's strikingly male features harden in response.

"Fridge—" she whispered, an icy filament of anxiety threading through her nervous system. Why had she felt compelled to mouth off? she demanded of herself with a flash of despair. Why hadn't she allowed him to enjoy his joke instead of challenging it?

Ralph Randall lifted his right hand. Although Keezia's heart and mind told her she had nothing to fear, an abuse-tutored voice from the darkest corner of her soul hissed otherwise.

She flinched inwardly, hating herself for doing so. The flinch was transmuted into a tremor of relief by the exquisitely gentle brush of Fridge's fingertips against her cheek.

"You're the first woman I've tried it out on," he said, his eyes boring deep into hers. She knew that he'd sensed her fear. She knew, too, that sensing it had hurt him. She added this hurt to the lengthy tally of her wrongs. "You're also the first woman besides my mama I've brought to this house." He stroked her cheek again, his touch clearly meant to soothe and reassure. "And I've never, ever cooked for another woman in my life."

"O-oh," she managed, the air seeming to leak from her lungs.

Fridge traced the shape of her mouth with the faintly calloused pad of his thumb. Her lips parted of their own volition. He slid his thumb between them, up to the first knuckle. Offering reassurance had obviously slipped down the list on his tactile agenda.

She sucked on him. Instinctively, at first. Then with deliberately sensual intent. She tasted a hint of Willie Leroy Randall's Coke-spiked barbecue sauce.

Fridge lifted her. Shifted her. Keezia couldn't follow the precise sequence of his fluent movements. She only knew that they ended with her sitting on his lap, her arms twined around his neck.

He nuzzled at the base of her throat for several seconds, then nibbled his way upward until he reached her mouth. They kissed. Long and deep. Deep and long. Keezia closed her eyes, seeing glittering explosions on the insides of her lids as her heart cartwheeled within her breast.

She wanted.

Oh, sweet heaven. *She wanted.*

Fridge lifted his lips from hers. She opened her eyes, whimpering at the loss. She was shaking.

"Keezia." Unlike his body, Fridge's voice was soft. "I've got fresh sheets on my bed and protection in the drawer next to it. I want to take you inside right now and make use of both of them. I want to love you tonight. And tomorrow. And the day after that. I want it so much I ache with it. But it's like the first time we kissed in your apartment. I need to be sure you want the same thing as I do."

"Say it, sugar," he'd urged her on a night more than six weeks past. *"Say it or show it. This is too important to both of us for me to be tryin' to read your mind."*

"Yes, Fridge," she told him. "Oh…yes!"

He undressed her as though she were the most precious gift he'd ever received, peeling back her garments with tender deliberation, lavishing praise on each and every newly bared inch of her body. He made her feel beautiful in ways she'd never dreamed possible.

He lingered over her lips for what could have been hours. Tasting. Testing. Teasing. Kissing her over and over and over. Feasting on her mouth as if it was the juiciest, ripest, most tempting piece of fruit since the apple in the Garden of Eden and he'd expire of starvation if he didn't get his fill of it.

She invoked his name on a shattered sigh, clutching at his broad shoulders. He groaned her name, deep in his throat. Their tongues twisted and twined, enticed and aroused.

"The more you give," he whispered hotly. "The more I need."

She made an instinctive attempt to shield her breasts with her hands as he undid and discarded the coffee-colored lingerie that had covered them. She was insecure about their shape and size. Fridge would not be forestalled. He eased her hands away and replaced them with his own.

"Perfect," he declared hoarsely, molding her with his warm palms. "So…perfect."

He stroked and gently squeezed. Caressed and finessed. He dipped his head and lapped at one nipple, then the other, coaxing the pebbled velvet peaks into tiny spiked crowns. When he finally took one between his lips, Keezia cried out with a pleasure that was as bright and sharp as a scalpel blade.

"I…want…" she whimpered.

"Whatever," he promised. "However. *Anything at all.*"

She took him at his word. And since what she wanted was to touch him, she did. Her first caress was tentative, but provoked a groan of undisguised pleasure. The second was a bit bolder. The third bolder still…

"*Yes,*" Fridge encouraged, the final consonant whistling through his gritted teeth. "Oh, baby. Oh…*yes.*"

There was so much for her to learn.

The sleek feel of his smooth, dark skin.

The nap and spring of his hair.

The salty tang and musky scent of his perspiration.

The sounds he made when she licked him…

And nipped at him…

And slowly, ever so slowly, curved her shaking fingers around the heat and hardness of him.

His big hands traveled over her body, kindling small bonfires of need that quickly escalated into hungry conflagrations. She twisted and trembled in response to his endless, irresistible wooing. Her heart was pounding like a trip-hammer. Her pulse performed a wildly syncopated fandango as her blood went storming through her veins.

He avoided the tight cluster of curls at the apex of her legs for what seemed a long, long time. In doing so, he made her achingly conscious of how desperately she wanted him to touch her there. When he finally slid his fingers between her thighs and found the petalled flesh that sheltered her feminine core, she was shocked by the convulsive intensity of her response. He caressed her with erotic thoroughness, gleaning the liquid essence of her readiness.

It was only when he shifted his body over hers in preparation for consummation that Keezia experienced a pang of panic. Her pulse stammered. She began to tense.

He was so…big.

So much stronger than she.

Even if he took all the care in the world—

Fridge sensed it. He was so attuned to her—so thoroughly under her skin, so deeply inside her head—that he seemed to realize what she was feeling at the same instant she did. Without uttering a word, he rolled over onto his back, taking her with him. The muscles in his arms rippled as he lifted her up, allowing her to straddle him. Stunned by the abrupt reversal of their positions, Keezia nearly pitched forward.

She used her hands to steady herself, pressing her palms flat against his sweat-slick chest. His heart was pounding even harder than hers. His breathing was as ragged as a runner's at the end of a marathon.

"I'm yours, Keezia," he declared thickly, stroking from her shoulders to her waist then cupping her slim hips. "Take as much as you want…and as long as you need."

She'd never thought of brown as a color capable of burning, but Ralph Booker Randall's dark eyes seemed to sear to the center of her soul as he uttered these words. The fear she'd felt less than a minute earlier went up in flames.

I'm yours, Keezia, he'd said.

And he was.

But she was his as well.

She knelt up, encircling Fridge with fingers that no longer shook. His hands tightened against her hips, helping her maintain her equilibrium but nothing more. Every muscle of his powerful body was rigid with the force of his self-restraint.

Take as much as you want…

All was what she wanted. No less would do. She claimed it in slow, sizzling increments, finally sheathing her lover to the hilt. She bit her lower lip as pressure began to build within her body. She arched her spine, straining toward release.

Fridge moved his hands up from her hips and cupped the underside of her small, conical breasts. He caught her pink-brown nipples between his thumbs and forefingers, tugging gently. An inarticulate cry broke from her lips as a red-hot burst of pleasure detonated deep within her.

…and as long as you need.

The world began to spin faster, then faster still. The passage of time accelerated in violation of every law of science.

"Oh…"

"Oh…yes."

Control frayed, then unraveled completely. Intimacy turned to flame. Ecstasy arrived in a firestorm of primal sensuality.

Keezia cried out Fridge's name in the same incandescent moment as he cried out hers. Their voices joined as one, as did their bodies.

The rightness of their coupling opened the way to a completion more powerful than either of them had ever known.

Six

Keezia slept afterward, cuddling trustingly against Fridge's chest and drifting off within the protective circle of his arms.

He remained awake for a long time. Watching over her. Absorbing the unique beauty of her face. Moonlight filtered in through the window to the left of the bed, bathing her luscious, creamed-coffee skin with a fairy-tale shimmer.

Lord, she was lovely!

The sweet curve of her forehead...

The elegant arch of her brows...

The delicate crescent of her feathered lashes, resting against her cheek...

And that mouth! So promising. So passionate. A saint would turn sinner for a taste of that mouth.

Keezia Lorraine Carew was his for the night and at least a day more. Fridge had wanted it to be that way the first time they made love. He'd *needed* it. Instinct had told him that no matter how good their initial coming together might be—and even in his wildest fantasizing he hadn't approached the ecstatic bliss of the joining he'd experienced a short time ago—the woman now lying in his arms would still try to retreat in the aftermath of it.

Having a 7:00 a.m. roll call to answer would have given her the perfect out. Other explanations of why she had to leave him he could have challenged. But not one involving her job as a firefighter. That area of her life was inviolable. Her work meant as much to her as his did to him.

Maybe more, in some ways.

He dipped his head, nuzzling against her earlobe and inhaling her heady feminine fragrance. He caught a hint of his own much funkier scent as he did so. A tremor jittered through him as he contemplated this evidence of their physical intimacy. He wondered hotly if his taste still lingered on her lips. One quick kiss and he could find out.

"Keezia," he whispered huskily, relishing the idea of his smell on her skin, his flavor on her mouth. "Oh, Keezia."

It had been like a knife to his heart when he'd felt her tense beneath him on the bed. But her panicked reaction had not been entirely unexpected. While he'd prayed with every shred of his soul that the demons from her past would leave her alone, he'd understood that the more willingly Keezia opened herself to him, the more vulnerable she became to the toxic legacy of her relationship with Tyrell Babcock.

If continuing to deny himself sexually had been the only antidote to her fear, he'd been prepared to go that route. He'd been ready to slow the pace of their lovemaking. To pull back and stop if necessary. To flat-out let Keezia go completely if bad turned to worst.

But it hadn't come to that. Thank God, it hadn't come to that at all. He'd ceded the woman he loved control and she'd taken it. The results had been his admission to a paradise on earth.

Keezia stirred, her eyelids twitching. She nuzzled at him, her tongue darting out to lick the knotted tip of his right nipple. Fridge sucked in a short, sharp breath, his muscles contracting. He heard her murmur something against his skin. A visceral shaft of satisfaction pierced him as he realized that the "something" was his name.

"Baby," he groaned, feeling the blunt rod of flesh between his thighs begin to rise.

His love of several years—and lover of several hours—stirred languidly. The bedsheets slipped down, revealing her small breasts to his gaze. The moonlight polished their mocha-colored curves with an alluring sheen. The cool from the softly humming air conditioner caused her nipples to crinkle into tight little rosettes.

And then Keezia's lashes fluttered up. She peered at him with warm, wondering eyes. The corners of her lush mouth began to curve. Fiery ribbons of anticipation unfurled in the pit of his belly.

"Fridge..." she said, seeming to savor the sound of his name.

The temptation to touch was too powerful to resist. Fridge caressed his bedmate with his hands and lips. She murmured his name again, her hips shifting in an ancient and evocative rhythm.

Eventually she reached for him, her desire very plain.

He reached for one of the foil packets on the nightstand, knowing that his pleasure would be false if he failed to protect her.

"Are you still mine, Ralph Randall?" Keezia asked throatily, reminding him of the pledge he'd offered in the face of her fears.

"Always," he vowed, then showed her what he meant.

Keezia awoke alone in a large, dark-sheeted bed in an airy, sunlight-filled room. It took her a moment to come to terms with where she was and what she was doing there.

"Oh," she breathed, her body responding to a sudden rush of memory. Her pulse scrambled. Her nipples stiffened. The tender flesh between her thighs throbbed and grew moist. "Oh...Fridge."

She'd never felt what she was feeling at this moment. Never felt what she'd felt in Fridge's arms last night. She'd never known that she was capable of doing so, if truth be told.

She'd given her virginity to the man she'd married. Not in

their honeymoon bed, though. No, she'd yielded the prize to Tyrell Babcock in the back seat of a secondhand Chevy nearly a year before their wedding night.

Tyrell had been her only lover until she'd shared herself with Ralph Booker Randall. Her ex-husband had frequently boasted that he'd made her a woman. She now understood that he'd lied about this as he'd lied about so much else. Whatever her abusive ex-husband had made of her—if, indeed, he'd "made" anything at all—had nothing to do with her sexuality.

His sexuality, perhaps. But definitely not hers. Because when all was said and done, Tyrell hadn't wanted a woman. Not a real one. Not the kind that she was struggling to be. He'd wanted a victim.

And Lord, had she been—

Keezia shoved this thought aside with a shudder and levered herself into a sitting position. Gathering an armful of sheets around her, she glanced at the clock on the bedside stand. The shock she got when she registered the time caused her hold on the linen to slacken.

10:42 a.m.? That was impossible! She hadn't slept in past seven in…in…well, she didn't know how long it had been. At least a year. Probably more. Her internal alarm clock wasn't calibrated to allow her to loll around in bed, frittering away potentially productive hours.

The word "loll" unleashed a rippling wave of sensual awareness in her. She shifted, once again conscious of the physical echoes of the previous night's lovemaking.

Who says lolling can't be productive? she asked herself, touching the tip of one breast with delicate deliberation. The responsive bud of flesh came to instant, aching attention. *If it isn't done alone, lolling might be very…*

Mmm.

She touched the tip of her other breast. Charted the circular shape of its silken areola. Shivered as a star-shower of self-induced pleasure cascaded down her body.

Yes.

It might be. *Very.*

A sudden yawn caught Keezia by surprise. She lifted her

right hand and covered her lips. She remembered making a similar gesture—for a different reason—the night Fridge had kissed her in the foyer of her apartment.

Her mouth had felt unfamiliar to her that night. Right now it felt...

Unfamiliar. Her entire body felt unfamiliar! But not in a frightening way. No, this unfamiliarity was a wonderous thing.

This is part of the truth about yourself, a small voice whispered. *It always has been. But you never trusted enough to*—

The door to the bedroom opened a bit. Fridge peered in. His lips parted in a smile when he saw that she was awake.

"Fridge!" she exclaimed, her voice soaring out of its normal alto range. She scrambled to pull the sheets up around her again. She managed to get her breasts covered, then realized the redraping had left her right leg bared to the hip.

"Hey, Sleeping Beauty," her lover of one night greeted her, opening the door a bit further. He was shoeless and shirtless, his only garment a skimpy pair of athletic shorts. He filled the entire space between the edge of the door and the frame. "I was beginnin' to think you were goin' to spend the entire day lollin' in bed."

Keezia felt herself flush. "Oh, n-no," she breathlessly denied, still struggling to rearrange the bed linen. Somewhere in the back of her mind she recognized that it was a little late in the day—in more ways than one—to be playing Miss Modesty. But that didn't stop her from trying. "I'd never do that."

Fridge lifted an eyebrow, letting his gaze wander from her eyes to her ankles and back again.

"Too bad," he commented. "I always thought lollin' in bed all day might be fun—"

Keezia gulped.

"—with the right person."

She gulped again, hoping her face didn't look as hot as it felt. It felt hot enough to fry an egg.

"It...it might be," she allowed after a moment or two. "With the right...person."

Fridge stretched like a jungle cat, the waistband of his shorts dipping below his navel to reveal most of a washboard-taut abdomen. He tugged the garment back into place without the slightest hint of embarrassment, then rotated his shoulders as though trying to work out some kinks. His muscles flexed and flowed with the limbering movements.

He was putting on quite a show. Keezia didn't know whether to avert her eyes or applaud. The option of urging him to take it off, take it al-l-l-l-l off also had a certain appeal.

"You always this agreeable in the mornin', sugar?" he finally asked, ambling over to the side of the bed.

She swallowed hard, ordering herself to get a grip. She was a fully grown woman, not some giggling schoolgirl. She had a brain in her head, not a bowl of mush. She could handle this situation. She could handle Fridge Randall. She could handle herself.

Keezia lifted her chin, reminding herself not to clutch too obviously at the sheets. "That depends."

Fridge seemed slightly surprised by this answer. Then one corner of his mouth kicked up. He nodded his head as though endorsing her less than definitive sentiment.

"Yeah," he concurred. "I suppose it does."

There was a pause.

"Um—" Keezia began.

Fridge forestalled her by bending forward and brushing a kiss against her slightly parted lips.

"Let me go get you some breakfast," he murmured. "You use the next couple of minutes to finish hidin' whatever part of you I'm not supposed to be lookin' at."

Keezia had herself back under control by the time her friend-turned-lover came back. She was in the midst of debating whether to snitch a T-shirt from Fridge's closet when she heard his footsteps coming down the hall. She dove for the bed, positioning a pair of pillows at her back and drawing the sheets up to her armpits.

"Come in," she called.

Fridge opened the door all the way this time. He entered the room carrying a food-laden tray. Keezia tried to tell herself that it was the scents wafting from it—not the sight of him—that made her mouth start to water. Innate honesty forced her to admit that it was both.

"First time I was ever invited into my own bedroom," he remarked mildly, crossing to the bed in a couple of long, lazy strides.

"Just making myself at home," Keezia returned, then bit her lower lip as she realized the full implication of her words. Her heart gave a strange hop-skip-jump. Oh, Lord. She hadn't meant—

"Glad to hear it," Fridge said, apparently accepting her comment as a no-hidden-meanings pleasantry. He placed the tray across Keezia's legs then sat down on the edge of the bed. Firm though it was, the mattress gave perceptibly under his weight.

Keezia shifted her position by a few inches, steadying the tray with one hand and struggling to make certain the bed linen stayed in place with the other. She avoided Fridge's gaze for several seconds, knowing the confusion she was experiencing must be obvious in her eyes. She was torn between a wish that she had sufficient sexual experience to be cool and casual and the realization that the idea of making love with any man other than Ralph Randall was repugnant to her.

"Sugar?"

She forced herself to look at him. His expression was impossible to read.

"What?"

He reached out and tucked the edge of the sheet behind her back. His touch made her senses sing.

"You were startin' to show again," he explained as he withdrew his hand.

Keezia mustered a little laugh.

"Not that I minded," he added, cocking his head. A hint of a smile eddied around the corners of his mouth. "Unless you've got somethin' underneath there I didn't get a chance to...see...last night."

Her breath hitched in her throat as she recalled the tender thoroughness of his lovemaking. Something he hadn't had a chance to see? He'd done everything but examine her with an electron microscope! And if there was a square centimeter of her he hadn't touched or tasted or both, she didn't know where it was located!

"Probably not," she conceded in a hushed, heated voice.

There was a pause. Lowering her gaze, Keezia plucked a napkin from the enticingly presented breakfast tray and began to unfold it.

"Maybe I should go," Fridge said quietly.

She lifted her head with a jerk. She'd messed up, she thought. No matter that she knew—*knew!*—she'd pleasured him the night before. That was then. This was now. And now was turning into an exercise in post-coital clumsiness courtesy of her own inept self.

"Why?" she asked.

As if she needed to. As if she couldn't run down a laundry list of reasons for herself.

"Because I'm obviously makin' you nervous, baby. You want some time to yourself. I understand. I knew I should give you some space this morning. But I waited so long for you to wake up—"

"No!" she protested as he started to rise. "No, please. Don't leave, Fridge. I'm not...nervous."

"You're not?"

She grimaced. "All right," she backpedalled, realizing that he wasn't going to let her get away with the pro forma denial. "Maybe I am. But not because of you. Because of *me!*"

Fridge reseated himself on the edge of the bed. He took a long, deep breath, then expelled it with equal deliberation. Finally, quietly, he asked, "Would you care to explain that to me, Keezia Lorraine?"

Care to?

No.

Need to?

Oh, yes. And maybe if she managed to explain it to him, she would find a way of making sense of it for herself.

"Sugar?" He used the tip of his right index finger to nudge her chin up.

"I'm not...good...at this, Fridge," she said.

"'This' bein'—what?"

She gestured, not wanting to detail her failures. "This!"

"You mean wakin' up in a man's bed after makin' love with him most of the night."

"Yes."

"I see." Fridge nodded slowly. "And what part of that particular 'this'—the wakin' up, the makin' love—are you laborin' under the impression you're not good at?"

The tenderness in his voice almost undid her. But she couldn't bear for him to pretend. "Except for Tyrell—"

He stoppered her lips with his fingers, a hint of temper flashing through his dark eyes.

"I don't want to hear about him, Keezia," he said harshly. "Not now. Not…this morning."

She eased back a little, wary of his sudden vehemence, yet determined to say what she believed needed to be said.

"Well, I don't want to talk about him, either," she countered, willing her voice to remain steady. "Not now. Not ever again. But I need you to know—to understand—that you're the only man besides him that I've been with. So if I don't know what to do or how to act—"

"Oh, baby," Fridge groaned, shaking his head. "Oh…baby."

She stared at him, her eyes flicking back and forth. She caught her breath.

"You knew, didn't you?" she finally whispered.

"Knew what? That I was your first since—" He refused to utter the name.

She nodded.

"No. Not for sure." His mobile mouth twisted. "But there was a part of me that…hoped. Which is same as sayin' there's a part of me that's pretty damned selfish where you're concerned."

"S-selfish?"

"You've told me what happened between you and—" again, the omission of the name "—out of bed. Well, I never imagined what happened *in* bed was much better. So to hope that that had been all you'd known until you and me...that's selfish.''

Her throat threatened to close up. She blinked rapidly against the pinprick sting of impending tears. "Oh, Fridge..."

"Now, don't go cryin' on me, sugar," he said hastily, picking up the napkin she'd unfolded and blotting gingerly beneath her eyes. "Please. Because if you want to talk about somebody not bein' *good* at somethin', you should see me tryin' to deal with a woman's tears!"

That there was a sliver of truth lurking behind this assertion was possible. But the exaggerated manner in which Fridge made his claim of incompetence was right over the top. Keezia's emotions veered, and what began as a choked sob became a hiccuping giggle.

"Here," she said after a moment, taking the napkin from Fridge. She felt a tingle run through her as their fingers brushed. "Let me mop my face."

"No need to mop," Fridge told her, the ease of his tone at odds with the expression in his eyes. "Just dab around here and there."

This time she laughed instead of giggled.

"Better?" she inquired after a judicious amount of dabbing.

Fridge smiled, the lines that bracketed his mouth indenting deeply. "Mighty fine."

Keezia replaced the napkin on her lap and made a show of surveying her breakfast tray. The offerings included a bowl of fresh berries, a stack of well-buttered toast, and a mug of black, not-quite-steaming coffee.

"This looks delicious," she said honestly. Then, feeling the need to keep things light, she raised her eyes to Fridge and added, "But it must have been a real ho-hum to fix."

He frowned. "Say what?"

Keezia batted her lashes. "Where's the danger?" she asked, harkening back to the ridiculous theory he'd spun for her the previous evening. "Unless, of course, you stole the berries from a field guarded by a bunch of gun-toting Klansmen and their rabid—"

"Oh, hush up," Fridge ordered, chuckling.

"What if I don't?"

"Then you won't get any chocolate cake."

Keezia's stomach rumbled.

"There's chocolate cake?" she asked, mentally licking her lips. She was a weak, weak woman when it came to chocolate. Why nutritionists didn't include it in the list of basic food groups was something she'd never understood. Unless maybe they thought "basic" wasn't emphatic enough.

Fridge chuckled again. "Unless you lied about what was in that pretty cardboard box you brought over yesterday, there's definitely chocolate cake."

That pretty cardboard—

Oh. Lord. She'd completely forgotten about that.

"Oh, right," she murmured. "The...dessert."

"Which we never got around to havin'."

Fridge's gaze slid downward as he spoke. Keezia darted a glance at her chest and made a quick tugging adjustment to the sheet.

"Not that I felt particularly deprived, you understand."

Topaz eyes met brown ones.

"I'm glad," she said after a few breathless seconds.

"In fact—" Fridge sketched a design on the fabric that covered her thigh "—I felt downright *satiated* when I woke up this mornin'."

Keezia held his gaze for a moment or two more, then applied herself to her breakfast. Her companion lapsed into silence but continued to stroke her upper leg through the bed linen.

"I think I could get used to this," she eventually observed, trying to ignore the jackrabbit jump of her pulse.

"It wouldn't take much to have the opportunity," Fridge replied, tracing a path down to her knee.

Keezia looked at him, puzzled.

"Just two words, sugar."

"Two...words?"

"Uh-huh."

"Mmm..." She pondered the problem, assuming this must be another flirtatious game. "Chocolate cake."

"Uh-uh."

Something streaked through the depths of his eyes that made her catch her breath. She went ahead and made a second playful guess anyhow.

"How about—'pretty please'?"

Ralph Booker Randall's hand stilled. His expression turned serious.

"No, sugar," he answered solemnly, his voice deep and resonant. "The two words are, 'I do.'"

Seven

"So he actually asked you to marry him."

Keezia suppressed a sigh. A mistake, she thought. Allowing herself to be conned into spending three days of her summer vacation with her supposedly ailing mother had been a mistake. Talking long distance, she could zig and zag around sensitive issues. Control the conversation to a certain extent. But talking face-to-face—

"Keezia?"

"What?"

"Don't 'what' me, young lady. This isn't like on the phone where you can pretend we've got a bad connection. Did Ralph Randall ask you to marry him last month?"

Keezia looked at the woman sitting next to her. Eloise Baxter was a handsome woman, with cinnamon-brown skin, salt-and-pepper hair and brandy-colored eyes. She was also a woman working on her fourth marriage. Her first had lasted six months. Her second, to Keezia's father, had lasted six years. Her third spin of the marital wheel had been blissfully lucky until her husband had tried to stop a robbery and been shot to death by a sixteen-year-old crackhead with a semi-automatic pistol.

Husband Number Four was Will Baxter of Memphis, Tennessee, who'd taken up teaching elementary school after retiring from the military. He and Eloise had wed more than eighteen months ago. But from what Keezia had observed, the happy couple was still in the honeymoon phase. In point of fact, her mother's alleged health problem apparently involved muscle strain due to conjugal overexertion.

"Yes, Mom," she confirmed quietly. "Fridge asked me to marry him last month." Twenty-nine days ago, it had been. And he'd followed up with a second proposal two weeks after the first.

"And you told him no."

"Not...exactly."

"Well, you certainly didn't tell him yes!"

"Mom, I've already gone through this with you. Hashing it over and over and over isn't going to accomplish anything."

"It might help me understand why."

Keezia almost laughed. She held the sound back because she knew it would come out sounding hateful and ugly. After a moment, she closed her eyes. A moment after that, she began remembering...

It had taken several seconds for the implications of Fridge's "two words" to sink in. At first, her brain had simply refused to accept that she'd heard what she'd heard. Or that the man who'd said what she refused to accept that she'd heard was serious.

"'I d-do'?" she'd finally stammered. Her heart had been beating so hard, she'd been afraid it might slam through her ribs. The spoon she'd been using to eat her breakfast berries had slipped from her fingers and dropped, clattering, against the tray. "You...you want me to m-marry you?"

Fridge had given her a strange look, then removed his hand from her leg. "Of course I want you to marry me."

"But—" She'd been riven by emotions she couldn't begin

to sort out. She'd been unprepared. Utterly, absolutely unprepared.

"But...what?" he'd pressed, his striking features taut. "You think all I want from you is...*this?*"

She'd trembled at his tone. *This,* she'd thought. How had he defined that word earlier, when her sexual insecurities had gotten the best of her? Something about her waking up in a man's bed after making love with him most of the night?

"What's wrong with...this?" she'd demanded, a little desperately. Why was he pushing? she'd wondered. They already had so much together! They were good, good friends. And after last night, it seemed that they were capable of being the best of lovers. To gamble what they had on *marriage*...

She couldn't. It wasn't that she didn't believe in the institution. She did. She'd seen living proof that it could work and work well. But for her—

"*You're my wife!*" she'd suddenly heard her ex-husband shouting. He was right in her face. She could see the rage in his eyes. Smell the sourness of his breath. Feel his spittle striking her bruised skin. "*My wife, Keezia! You know what that means?*"

Oh, yes. She'd known. She'd had the knowledge beaten into her.

Fridge Randall isn't Tyrell Babcock, the little voice that previously had counseled her to trust had suddenly whispered. Never was. Never will be.

She knew that. Believed that. But she also knew that she—

"There's nothing wrong with 'this,'" Fridge had responded at that point, dragging her out of the past.

"Then why—"

He'd stood up abruptly, looking every inch of his six-foot-four-inch height—and then some. "I didn't wait three long years just to screw you, Keezia Lorraine!"

It had been the crudest thing she'd ever heard him say. Had he hauled off and belted her across the face, she might have been less shocked. Her expression must have revealed the turbulence of her reaction, because he'd suddenly looked ill.

"I'm sorry," he'd said, his voice low and strained. He'd

started to reseat himself on the edge of the bed, then aborted the movement as though fearing she'd flinch away from him. He'd clenched and unclenched his big, blunt-fingered hands several times. "Lord help me. I'm sorry. I didn't mean—"

"Yes, you did," she'd contradicted, suddenly very certain of herself.

"Keezia—"

She'd patted the mattress, holding his gaze steadily, wordlessly communicating that she wasn't afraid to have him near. After another hesitation, he'd accepted her invitation and sat down. He'd made no effort to touch her.

"Three years?" she'd finally asked.

He'd taken a deep breath. Expelled it very slowly. "From the moment my mama introduced us."

"Oh, Fridge."

"I love you, sugar."

"And I—" A knot had formed in her throat. She'd swallowed convulsively. Then she'd reached out and laid her right hand on top of his. She'd felt him stiffen at the contact. "I l-love you, too."

"But not enough to marry me?"

She'd shaken her head. "It's not a question of *enough*, Fridge."

"Then what is it a question of?" He'd clasped her hand between both his own and lifted it to his lips, feathering a kiss across her knuckles.

"I'm not…ready."

An emotion she hadn't been able to identify had flickered through the depths of his compelling brown eyes. "But you could be, someday."

Her heart had lurched. She'd felt a flash of panic. Where it had come from, she hadn't known. But she'd responded to it by sidestepping his assertion and retreating to what had become the mantra of their relationship.

"I need time."

He'd studied her for several poignant moments, his expression impossible to read. Keezia's confidence had begun to ebb, flowing out of her like water from an unplugged sink.

What if her time had run out? she'd asked herself uneasily. He'd already spoken of waiting three long years.

Dear God. What if Fridge decided that if she wouldn't give him all, he'd walk away with nothing?

The question had sprung to her lips, tasting of what seemed like a pathetic degree of neediness. She'd tried to choke it back but had failed.

"Will you still want to…b-be…with me if I don't—?"

Again, an emotion she couldn't put a name to had stirred in his eyes. Then, astonishingly, his mouth had twisted into a rueful smile.

"You mean, am I strong enough to resist the temptations of the flesh outside the bonds of holy matrimony?" he'd countered.

Well, yes. And…no. It wouldn't have occurred to her to define the issue in such biblical-sounding terms. Then again, it wouldn't have occurred to her that Fridge Randall might feel some ambivalence—maybe even some guilt—about engaging in premarital sex.

She'd nodded.

He'd released her hand, then stroked the side of her face. It was a lover's touch. Slow. Sensual. Deeply appreciative. After a few seconds, he trailed his fingertips down the line of her throat, bringing them to rest in the sensitive hollow where he could gauge the throb of her pulse.

"No, baby, I'm not that strong," he'd answered simply. "Not where you're concerned."

"I'm not the first woman you've had." Although she'd felt a twist of jealousy as she'd made the assertion, that hadn't been her primary reason for making the point. She'd known from their first meeting that Fridge Randall was a man of depth and character. But the past few minutes had shown her that he was far more complex than she'd realized.

"No," he'd quietly affirmed. He'd started to withdraw his hand. She'd forestalled him, placing her hand on top of his. He'd resisted for the space of a heartbeat, then begun caressing her again. "Though that's not somethin' I'm particularly proud of."

"I wouldn't expect—"

"I understand that. But there's a part of me that thinks the idea of savin' yourself for marriage shouldn't just be put on women. Unfortunately, there's another part that gets a little...carried away...under certain circumstances."

Keezia had felt her own mouth curve at this point. A voluptuous shiver had coursed through her nearly naked body. Her toes had curled beneath the sheets. "Or a *lot* carried away."

"It was good for you last night?" The question had held a mix of egotism and insecurity. A contradictory combination, to be sure. But very, very human.

"I never knew, Fridge," she'd told him, trusting the expression on her face and the emotion in her voice would make up for her lack of eloquence. She really didn't have the words to describe the beauty of what she'd experienced with him. "What I felt when we made love...*I just never knew.*"

He'd nodded, his eyes very dark. Then he'd leaned in and pressed a kiss to her lips. She'd kissed him back, quivering as she felt the coaxing stroke of his tongue.

"It's not goin' to go away, Keezia," he'd whispered, lifting his mouth from hers. "I'll keep on bein' your friend and your lover. Only that's not my bottom line. I want to be your husband. I want to be a daddy to the children you said you wanted to have. But if you need more time—"

"—Tyrell Babcock?"

The sound of her mother's voice uttering her ex-husband's name jerked Keezia back into the present. She experienced a moment or two of queasy-stomached disorientation.

"W-what?" she stammered.

This time, her mother didn't accuse her of trying to evade the subject at hand. Eloise Baxter wrinkled her forehead instead, her artfully made-up eyes clouding with a combination of anxiety and sorrow.

"I asked if it's Tyrell Babcock that's keeping you from saying yes to Ralph Randall," she answered.

The queasiness came back, escalating to something close to nausea. Keezia gulped for air.

"You think—" her stomach roiled *"—I still have feelings for him?"*

Her mother looked horrified. "No, honey! Oh, no!" she cried, shaking her well-coiffed head in vehement denial. "Of course not."

"Then how could you ask—?"

"I only meant to suggest that what he did to you might have—have—"

"What? Left me with permanent brain damage?" Keezia knew that there was something off-kilter about her reaction. The words she was flinging at her mother were truly vile. But she couldn't seem to stop them. She felt that she was defending herself against some unseen enemy, engaged in a fight for her very life.

"That son of a bitch did you a whole lot of hurt, honey," her mother responded, her voice low but shaking with fury. "The kind of hurt it can take a long, long time to heal. And maybe, just maybe, you're afraid Ralph Randall might—"

"No." Keezia shook her head. She wasn't. She *wasn't* afraid of Fridge!

But she was afraid of something.

Of…someone?

"Then why, Keezia?" Eloise Baxter asked. "Why can't you say yes to the man?"

"I don't know, Mom." Or if she did, she didn't know she knew. "I just can't. Not…yet."

"But you love him."

Keezia blinked several times. The bridge of her nose congested with the pressure of unshed tears. "Yes."

"And he loves you."

"Y-yes."

"Oh, baby." Her mother scooted over on the couch they were sharing and put her arms around Keezia. "There, there. Don't cry. Things will work out. I just know with all my heart that they will. All you have to do is give them some time."

Keezia gave a weak, watery laugh and leaned her head

against her mother's shoulder. It had been a long while since she'd let herself be babied this way. The last time might have been the night she'd found the courage—if courage was the right word—to leave Tyrell Babcock for good.

Her mother rubbed her back with gentle, soothing strokes, crooning wordlessly. After a while she asked, "Have I told you how proud I am of everything you've done the last few years?"

Keezia smiled, moved by the compliment. "I don't mind being told more than once."

"Well, I am. Very proud."

"Thanks, Mom."

They sat in silence for a minute or so. Eventually Eloise Baxter said, "I'd like a chance to get to know this Fridge of yours."

Keezia's heart skipped a beat. She sat up slowly, knuckling away the dampness under her eyes. "I'm sure he'd like to get to know you, too."

"That one time I met him when I came to visit you in Atlanta...I could tell he was a good man."

"He is, Mom."

"You deserve that, honey. You deserve a good man."

To this, Keezia Lorraine Carew said nothing.

"Hey, Keez!"

Keezia checked her step and pivoted in the general direction of this shouted greeting. A moment later, she spotted J.T. Wilson plowing through the gathered throng. He had a pretty young black woman by the hand. Mitch Jones trailed behind, wolfing down a hot dog.

"Hey, J.T.," she said when the trio reached her. "Hey, Mitch."

"Mmmph, mumphzee," Mitch responded through a mouthful of food.

Keezia glanced at J.T.'s companion. She got a chilly once-over in return and experienced a flash of doubt about the wisdom of the outfit she'd chosen to wear to this, the Atlanta Fire Department's annual Show and Muster. Her mother had taken her shopping while she'd been in Memphis and she'd fallen in love with a sleeveless, tightly belted jumpsuit that was almost as yellow as the stripes that banded the chest and cuffs of her black firefighter's turnout jacket. The garment was a lot more…obvious…than her usual attire.

Well, so what if it was? she rallied herself a moment later, straightening her spine. She'd seen herself in the store mirror. She had the shape to wear something twice this snug! Anyway. She'd zipped the jumpsuit on with an eye toward having Fridge peel it off. Who cared what some prissy, prejudiced female she'd never met thought of it?

"Oh, yeah," J.T. said, apparently remembering his manners. "Keezia, this is my fiancée, Lucinda Dupree. Cinda, this is Keezia Carew. The female firefighter? The one on my shift? I know I've mentioned her, baby—"

"How do you do, Miz Carew," Lucinda said. She inclined her head an ungracious inch or two. Considering how stiff her neck looked, Keezia was surprised she managed that much movement.

"I do just fine, Miz Dupree," she returned, suppressing an urge to roll her eyes. She was accustomed to having awkward first encounters with her co-workers' wives and girlfriends. She generally went out of her way to try and charm them. But in this case…

"So, where have you been?" Mitch asked after gulping down the remainder of his hot dog.

"Visiting my mom in Memphis."

"Too bad you missed the competition," J.T. said. "Our station won the Fun Firefighters' trophy again."

"No kidding!"

"We swept everything from bucket brigadin' to hose layin'," Mitch boasted. "We kicked butt."

"J.T.—"

"In a second, baby," J.T. promised, flashing his wife-to-be a quick smile. Keezia suspected he'd regret the brush-off. "Actually, Keez, it was Jackson and Fridge who kicked most of the butt."

Knowing her colleague was looking for a reaction, Keezia

disciplined herself to seem interested but not too interested in this tidbit. While she didn't delude herself that her involvement with Fridge had gone unnoticed in the department, she didn't want to provide any more grist for the gossip mill than she had to.

"I'm sorry I missed that," she answered.

"Keezia's got a thing going with Fridge Randall," J.T. said to his girlfriend. "You know? The big stud with the fine mustache I introduced you to after the competition?"

Although Keezia was not particularly pleased at having her private business bandied about, she was amused to note that Cinda the Stiff-Necked seemed to thaw a couple of degrees in the wake of this information.

"Oh," the young woman said, giving Keezia another up-down-up assessment. "You and Ralph Randall go out?"

"At least once a week," drawled a familiar male voice. "And sometimes they stay in."

It was Bobby Robbins, accompanied by his Asian-American wife, Mai. Mai was pushing a stroller. Lying in the stroller was a goo-gooing baby girl with dark, tip-tilted eyes and an adorable fluff of light brown hair.

There was another round of greetings and introductions, followed by the requisite admiring of little Iris Robbins. Keezia bent over the stroller, tickling the baby's sweetly rounded tummy. She felt an unexpected pang of yearning when Iris latched onto one of her fingers and didn't seem to want to let go.

"She likes you, Keez," Bobby said, chuckling.

"That's because she's a baby with very good sense," Mai declared, giving Keezia a warm smile. Keezia smiled back. Mai Robbins was one woman who'd accepted her right from the start.

"Brains as well as beauty?" J.T. gibed. "Geez, Bobby, what'd she inherit from you?"

"J.T.!" Cinda looked shocked.

"Never mind him," Keezia and Mai said simultaneously. Then they looked at each other and laughed.

"What's the matter?" J.T. asked his fiancée, obviously puzzled by her reaction.

"Oh, nothin'," Bobby responded before the young woman could get a word in edgewise. "She's just reconsidering the wisdom of marryin' you."

This assertion provoked a minute or so of crosstalk. Keezia listened to the back-and-forth banter with half an ear, devoting most of her attention to scanning the hurly-burly crowd around her.

Where was Fridge? she wondered, nibbling her lower lip. Why couldn't she spot him? It wasn't as though the man was inconspicuous! He always stood—

"He's over at the picnic tables," Mitch said.

Keezia started. "What?"

"Fridge. That's who you're lookin' for, right?"

She couldn't deny it. Well, actually, she could, but no one except Baby Iris would believe her.

"Yeah, Mitch," she confirmed. "I'm looking for Fridge."

"Well, like I said, he's over there—" Mitch pointed "—at the picnic tables under the trees. We saw him about ten minutes ago."

"That's right," J.T. put in. "He was with Jackson. And guess who *Jackson* was with?"

"Uh—"

"That red-haired Yankee headshrinker he's got livin' under his roof."

Keezia's trek to the picnic tables was a stop-start thing. She kept encountering people she knew, which naturally mandated she stand and make polite conversation for a minute or so before excusing herself and moving on.

She found Fridge—and Jackson and Jackson's "red-haired Yankee headshrinker"—exactly where she'd been advised to look. Her first impulse was to call out a greeting. Then she decided to opt for a more stealthy approach. She wanted to have a chance to assess Dr. Phoebe Donovan before she actually met her.

Jackson Miller's tenant was tall and willowy, with red-gold

hair and milk-pale skin. She exuded a cool, classy intelligence. She was dressed in a pristine white T-shirt and a crisp pair of navy blue shorts. She also seemed to be having a very good time. As a matter of fact, the woman appeared to be laughing so hard she was crying.

"Please...stop," Keezia heard her plead as she moved within earshot.

"Oh, man, Jackson," Fridge chortled from the other side of the table. He was clad in jeans and an orange T-shirt emblazoned with the words Hot Stuff. The sight of that physique-flaunting top made Keezia decide that her yellow jumpsuit was just fine. "Do you remember how Chuckie Fremont wound up all over the local news that night?"

Keezia started to smile. She should have guessed that they'd get around to regaling Dr. Donovan with the candy-coated saga of Charles Herdon Fremont. It was more than a story. It was a department legend.

"Yeah, and he made the front page of the *Atlanta Constitution,* too," Jackson said. "It looked like he'd been tarred and—"

"Let me guess," Keezia spoke up, moving forward. "You two fun firefighters are torturing this poor woman with the story of charging Chuckie Fremont and the chocolate syrup."

Fridge got to his feet in a smooth surge, his teeth showing white beneath his mustache. He took in her choice of attire with a sweeping gaze, then gave her a three-alarm look of approval.

"Sister Carew," he said, his voice rich and rumbling.

"Hey, Keezia," Jackson seconded, standing up as well.

Glancing out of the corner of her eye, Keezia thought she saw Phoebe Donovan's eyes narrow.

"I thought you were still in Memphis with your mama," Fridge commented.

"I drove back overnight."

"She's feelin' better, then?"

"Enough to start nagging me about when I'm going to come to my senses and settle down with you," Keezia answered, setting her earrings swinging with a toss of her head. The response came out with more of an edge than she'd intended. She was still unsettled by the conversation she and her mother had had about Fridge. She was also discomforted by the way Jackson's headshrinker seemed to be staring at her. Deciding that it might be wise to confront the latter challenge head-on, she turned and said, "Dr. Phoebe Donovan, am I right?"

The other woman looked, strangely, more than a little embarrassed. She even started to flush. Then she seemed to reach down inside herself and press some kind of "poise" button. Suddenly, she was back in control.

"Yes," she replied in a beautifully modulated voice. "And you're obviously Keezia Carew, the firefighter."

Keezia stiffened, uncertain what to make of this response. She looked from the redhead to Jackson to Fridge. Was it possible that her lover had decided to consult—

"Has somebody been talking behind my back?" she demanded.

"Not me." Fridge shook his head. He seemed genuinely surprised by Phoebe's words.

"Me, either," Jackson echoed, giving his tenant an odd look. "How the heck did you—"

"Lauralee," Phoebe Donovan said simply, then returned her attention to Keezia.

The redhead smiled at her. Not a lot, but enough to make a genuine impression. Keezia found herself starting to smile back. She'd never been big on forming friendships with other females. But there was something about this woman...

"Jackson's daughter, Lauralee, mentioned your name to me," Phoebe explained. "She's a big admirer of yours, Ms. Carew. She thinks you're a very independent woman."

"Mmm..."

"There?"

"A little bit—yeah." Fridge made a sound that was part pain, part pleasure, as Keezia kneaded a spot about halfway down his spine. "Oh, *yeah*. Right there."

"You're very tight."

"I think—" he stifled a groan as Keezia flexed her fingers

against his flesh ''—I got a little too intent on makin' sure our station kept the trophy.''

His companion gave a husky laugh. A moment later, he felt her warm breath fan his ear.

"Maybe you're getting too old to be a Fun Firefighter," she suggested provocatively.

He growled in mock outrage and flipped their positions in a single, seamless movement. But even as he executed the impulsive move, he was careful not to exert his physical dominance too obviously. He'd never forgotten the panicked tension he'd felt in Keezia's body the first night they'd made love.

"You want to say that again?" he challenged silkenly, gauging the expression in his partner's beautiful topaz-gold eyes. She looked excited, not apprehensive. And despite a fair amount of squirming, she was making no real effort to free herself.

They were in the bedroom of Keezia's Virginia Highlands apartment. They'd left the Show and Muster about two hours ago, heading to her place after a brief stop at his house to pick up Shabazz. The neighbor who usually checked on the cat while Keezia was on duty was away on a cruise, and she'd been uneasy about leaving the feline to fend for herself while she went to Memphis. Fridge had volunteered to play cat sitter. Although he'd ended up being cat-*sat* upon on several occasions—Shabazz had woken him out of a sound sleep by cannonading onto the center of his chest three different times—things had gone pretty well.

One thing had led to another once they'd arrived at her apartment and they'd ended up making love in the shower. They'd eventually adjourned to the bedroom, where Keezia had offered to massage what he'd offhandedly described as his aching back.

Keezia laughed a second time. The throaty sound had an unsettling effect on Fridge's already uneven pulse. Likewise, the sight of her nipples thrusting against the fabric of his orange Hot Stuff T-shirt. She'd appropriated the garment for her own use when they'd left the bathroom.

"Careful," she warned. "Maneuvers like that can be dangerous to a Fun Firefighter."

"Only—" he stroked a hand up her ribcage and palmed her right breast "—if the Fun Firefighter doesn't observe standard safety precautions."

He lowered his head. She cupped the back of his neck. They kissed. A long, lingering kiss, with lots of tongue and teeth.

Keezia exhaled on a languid sigh when they finally eased apart. Her color was high. Her eyes were full of heat. "I guess this means your back has stopped aching?"

Fridge smiled. He shifted, letting her feel the resurgence of his need. "The ache I have right now isn't in my back, sugar."

She reached up and caressed his cheek. After a few seconds he turned his face into her palm and kissed it. Her skin was smooth, but it wasn't soft. She worked too hard for that. She had competent, capable hands. Although he suspected she'd disbelieve it if he told her, this was one of the reasons he found her touch so intensely arousing.

"What do you think of Phoebe Donovan?" she asked, running a teasing fingertip along the edge of his mustache. He'd asked her several weeks ago whether she liked the feel of it on her skin. Her response had been a smile that had sent his temperature soaring.

"Well—" Fridge paused, trying to make room in his Keezia-crammed consciousness for an opinion about another woman. After a few seconds he shifted their positions again, hoping this would make it easier to keep his libido on hold. "I think she's an interestin' woman. Smart about people. But she keeps a lot inside. I also think she's got somethin' goin' with Jackson, only neither one of 'em is exactly sure what it is yet."

"Hmm."

"What did you think of her?" He was genuinely curious. Although the first couple of minutes of their Show and Muster encounter had looked dicey to him, he'd sensed a real affinity between Keezia and Phoebe by the time they'd finally parted.

"Well, there was a second or two when I thought you might have…discussed…me with her."

The fractional hesitations bracketing the verb told Fridge precisely what kind of "discussing" Keezia had suspected. He shook his head.

"I wouldn't do that, sugar," he said quietly.

His bedmate sighed. "I know you wouldn't. I *knew* you wouldn't, even when I was thinking you might have—if that makes any sense."

Fridge said nothing. What could he say? The woman he loved—and who said she loved him—was still struggling to learn to trust with both her head and her heart.

"My second thought—or maybe it was my first, I'm not sure—was that Phoebe was reacting to me like so many other firefighters' wives and girlfriends and...whatevers."

"You thought she thought you might be after Jackson." It was something he and Keezia had talked about before. Until she'd informed him otherwise, he'd always assumed that other women showed her a you-go-girl attitude because of her achievements. He'd discovered that the so-called "sisterhood" could be pretty nasty to a female who had the independence to push her way into a man's world.

"I've told you how it is. A lot of women worry that I can't do the job physically and might be a threat to their men because of it. That I can handle."

Fridge ran his palms down her sleekly muscled arms. "By lettin' 'em know you run—what is it now? Forty miles a week? And work out at the gym with weights."

"Exactly. I can even deal with the women who get jealous. I mean, most of the time the men they're so possessive of are firefighters I wouldn't want to ride on the same truck with, much less—"

"*Most* of the time?"

Keezia gave him a very female look, obviously not entirely displeased by this brief flash of jealousy. "Ninety-nine and nine-tenths percent of the time."

He nodded. "Just checking."

"Anyway. The ones who really get to me are the women who act as though any female who'd become a firefighter is a slut—wanting to sleep and shower in a fire station with a bunch of men.''

''You shouldn't bother about folks who're too blind to see the truth about you, baby.'' He shifted his position again, bringing their bodies back into intimate alignment.

He watched Keezia's eyes cloud as he slipped his hand between her naked thighs. He stroked upward, rubbing gently against her delicate female flesh. She rocked her pelvis once. Twice. The feel of her was all wet warmth and welcome.

''What...what is the truth...about me?''

Fridge used his other hand to tug the orange T-shirt up, baring her breasts. He knew she thought they were small. He thought they were the perfect size and shape. They fit his palms as though they'd been created for them.

''That you're—'' he kissed one corner of her mouth ''—an independent—'' he kissed the other ''—woman.''

He entered her in the same moment he claimed the center of her lips, joining them with a smooth, sure stroke. He drank in the cry she made as she arched up, taking him even deeper into her body.

They moved together. Slowly at first, as though they had all the time in the world. Then faster. And faster.

He cupped his hands beneath Keezia's bottom, pulling her closer. He couldn't get enough of her.

''Please...'' she moaned, the brief bite of her nails urging him on. ''Oh, please.''

''Soon,'' he promised, his lips pulling back from his teeth as he strained forward a few critical centimeters. He felt so hot. As though the core of his being was on fire. He wondered fleetingly whether those tabloid tales of spontaneous human combustion might be true.

Fridge was teetering on the edge of ecstasy, using every shred of discipline at his command to restrain himself from succumbing to its incendiary promise of pleasure, when he felt the rippling tug that signaled the start of Keezia's release. He thrust one last time and drove both of them into the waiting flames.

Eight

Two weeks after the Show and Muster, Fridge came down with the flu. He endured the ailment stoically for a day or so, but by the end of forty-eight hours he was sick of being sick. And the sicker he got of it, the sicker he felt.

Bad enough that he'd had to miss a day's work for the first time in close to eight years. He'd also been forced to cancel a long-scheduled visit to a local day camp. The visit was part of a community outreach project run by the Department of Public Safety. Participants went into classrooms to talk about fire prevention, home safety and personal responsibility.

Fridge been asked to volunteer for the program about five years back, but had been hesitant about signing up. He wasn't certain how he'd deal with a mob of little kids. Although he'd worked with teenagers through his church and found the experience both challenging and rewarding, he hadn't had much hands-on experience with the under-ten set.

Eventually, however, he'd agreed to give it a try. He'd ended up having a terrific time. When the students had clamored for him to make a return appearance, he'd been happy to agree. And when he'd learned several weeks later that one of the fourth graders he'd spoken to had used the tips he'd offered to save herself and two younger siblings from a fire in the apartment where they'd been left alone...

Happy didn't begin to describe how he'd felt about that. He'd known he'd been positively blessed.

"Ah-*choo*," he sneezed, barely getting the soggy mass of tissue he was holding in his right hand up to his mouth and nose in time to cover them. He mopped his sore and streaming nostrils for several seconds, then heaved the sodden fistful of paper into the wastebasket at the side of his bed. The clock on the nightstand read 6:03 a.m.

Keezia bustled in, carrying a large glass of orange juice in one hand and a mug of some kind of steaming liquid in the other. She was immaculately dressed in her dark blue firefighter's uniform. While the cut of the shirt and trousers was supposed to be asexual, it flattered her lithe, well-toned figure. This was supposed to be a day off for her, but she'd been called to come in because of an unusually large number of illness-related absences.

"That didn't sound very good," she commented, clucking her tongue.

"Don't worry," Fridge grumped. "It'll get better with practice."

At least that's what he intended to say. Even allowing for the hearing distortion caused by the congested condition of his ears, he knew the statement came out sounding more like: "Dobe wowwy, id'll geh bedduh wih p'actis."

Keezia set the glass and the mug down on the bedside stand, one corner of her curvy mouth indenting as though she were trying to hold back a laugh. Fridge observed the tiny twitch with a sense of indignation. *Fine thing,* he told himself. *Makin' fun of a sick man.*

"The juice is fresh-squeezed," she announced in what seemed like an inappropriately cheerful tone. "I made a whole pitcherful for you. It's in the refrigerator, along with that pot of chicken soup I cooked up. The tea's herbal, by the way."

Fridge grimaced at the last bit of information. "Herbal? Stuff tastes like boiled weeds!"

The woman he wanted to marry straightened, giving him one of those slightly amused, superior-female-to-pathetically-suffering-male looks. He dimly remembered his mama surveying his daddy with exactly the same expression when Willie Leroy Randall had been laid low with a wicked case of poison ivy. He wondered if such looks were genetically programmed or some sort of hormonal thing.

"If you can taste it, you must be getting better," Keezia countered sweetly. "Yesterday you swore you could drink a spicy cocktail with a jalapeño chaser and not taste a thing."

Fridge tried to summon up a sardonic little laugh to let his lover know how tacky he thought it was for a healthy woman to be using an ailing man's words against him. Unfortunately, the first "ha-ha" jammed in the middle of his scratchy throat and turned into a coughing fit that somehow metamorphosed into a series of spasming sneezes.

"Auuurgh," he groaned, collapsing back against the pillows when the hacking and achoo-ing finally subsided. There was a miserable ache in his bones. His chest felt sore, too, as though Shabazz had been using it as a trampoline.

"Oh, honey," Keezia crooned, suddenly all sympathy. She leaned over and stroked his forehead with her cool, competent hands. Then she dipped her head and brushed a kiss against his temple. For a crazy instant, he thought he could smell her slightly spicy scent. "I'm sorry you've got this bug so bad."

Fridge gazed up at her with bleary eyes. His weakness annoyed—no, it downright disgusted him. Still, he had to admit that there was something nice about being pampered, fussed over and waited on by a beautiful woman. Aside from her efforts to keep pouring vile-flavored hot toddies into him and an occasional muttered comment about how men acted like big babies when they took ill, Keezia had been an absolute angel of mercy since he'd taken sick.

Maybe this was the way to finally get through to her, he suddenly found himself musing. Maybe seeing him so wretched and vulnerable would soften her continued resistance to his—

Fridge stopped, ripping this line of thought out by the roots and casting it away. He was utterly appalled at himself. What in the name of Heaven had possessed him to consider such a possibility? he wondered, his temples starting to throb. The last thing in the world he wanted was for Keezia Lorraine Carew to accept his marriage proposal out of *pity!* Better she keep asking for more "time" because of some misplaced fear than that.

"Fridge?" Keezia questioned, caressing his forehead again. She studied him with undisguised concern. "Baby? What's wrong?"

"Nothing," he insisted hoarsely. "I'm fine."

"You don't look fine." She clucked her tongue again and frowned, a vertical line creasing the skin between her eyebrows. "You know, I think your mama was right. The medicine you're taking isn't doing you much good. Maybe you should go see the doctor again and—"

"No!"

The negative exploded out of him. It was followed by an industrial-strength sneeze that seemed to detonate somewhere in the center of his chest and spew upward. He fumbled for more tissues, bringing another fistful to his nose. After about fifteen seconds of blowing and snuffling he finally felt ready to resume speaking.

"I don't need to go back to the doctor," he declared. He'd already endured his mama nagging him half to death about making another appointment when she'd come to check up on him yesterday afternoon. He didn't need Keezia pushing the same routine. Professionally, he held medical people in the highest esteem. Personally, though, he preferred to steer clear of them. He was wary about hospitals, too. He couldn't set foot in one without thinking about his father's long and painful battle with cancer.

"But—"

"No—" he coughed "—doctors!"

"All right! All right!" Keezia held up her slender-fingered

hands in mock-surrender. "No doctors." She glanced at the bedside clock and pulled a face. "Oh, Lord. Look at the time. I've got to run, Fridge."

"Go, baby," he urged, burying his abused nose in the wad of tissues he'd snatched up. "I'll be okay."

Keezia dropped another quick kiss on the top of his head, then headed off to answer her seven a.m. roll call.

After chugging down most of the orange juice, Fridge drifted into a light sleep. He snoozed restlessly for about an hour, finally jolting himself out of his slumberous state with a shattering sneeze. He stared at the ceiling for an uncomfortable minute or so, breathing raspily through his mouth, then hauled himself out of bed and padded into the bathroom. He took care of a number of items of business in there—including pouring the rust-colored herbal tea into the john and flushing it away—then wobbled back to bed.

A search through the sheets turned up the remote control to the small TV he had sitting on the bureau positioned against the wall to the right of the bed. He clicked the set on, then surfed through the channels until he came to a news report. He listened for a few minutes, then crankily decided that it was basic déjà vu—a scandal in Washington, trouble in the Mideast, some lobbying group claiming that yet another one of life's pleasures was potentially dangerous to people's health—and surfed on. He ended up watching some British-made nature show about the cycle of life on the Serengeti.

The program's closing credits were just beginning to roll when the phone rang. Fridge's first impulse was to let the answering machine take care of it. But something—a nasty little tickle in the back of his brain—compelled him to pick up.

"Ahh-ahh-*choo*," he sneezed into the receiver. The bedside clock said 7:24 a.m. He wondered how Keezia was doing at the fire station. While he had no doubts about her professional abilities, he knew from experience that working with an unfamiliar crew could be difficult.

"Fridge?"

It was Keezia. There was an edge to her voice that affected him like a super-antibiotic. His ears, nose and chest suddenly unclogged.

"Here, sugar," he said, sitting up.

"Is Jackson there?"

"Jackson?" He frowned, knowing his friend had come off shift at the same time she'd gone on. "No, he's sure not. Why?"

"The station caught a call on a residential fire early this morning, a couple of hours before the end of the A shift. A bunch of apartments. There was a casualty. A baby girl. Smoke inhalation, probably, because she wasn't burned. Jackson went in and brought her out."

No, Fridge thought, a spasm of sadness racking him. He closed his eyes. *Dear Lord…no.*

No death was easy for a firefighter to accept. But the loss of a child was the most difficult to bear. With an adult, there was the comfort of the thought that at least he or she had had some time to live, some time to know human happiness. With a little one…

Fridge had helped to pull the body of a dead child out of fire while he was still a probie. The image of that child was like a scar on his brain. He knew he would see it in nightmares until the end of his days.

"Fridge?"

He opened his eyes. "Still with you, baby. Did you hear about this from Jackson?"

"Uh-uh. I saw him for a few seconds at the shift change, though. He looked bad, Fridge. Really drained. And he had that seen-too-much stare, you know? Somebody said the captain tried to talk him into calling one of the department counselors, but he turned the idea down flat and said he was clocking out. I thought he might come by to see you. To…discuss…things."

Fridge exhaled on a long, weary breath. "Well, if that's his intention, he hasn't made it here yet. But I'll be on the watch for him. And I'll try phonin' his house, too."

"Good." Keezia paused for a moment, then cleared her

throat. "There's one other thing about the baby that died, Fridge. Somebody said they thought her name was Anne."

"Oh...no."

"That was his wife's name, wasn't it?"

"Yeah." Fridge shook his head grimly, feeling for his friend. "Anne...with an *e*."

"Makes it that much worse."

"You've got that right." Jackson had lost his wife to cancer eight years ago, when Lauralee was just seven. Fridge sometimes thought that the bravery his friend demonstrated as a firefighter was less impressive than the courage he'd shown in the wake of his wife's untimely death.

Keezia sighed. "Well, I just thought you should know. So you could...reach out to him, or something."

"I appreciate your callin'. I truly do."

"Are you feeling any better?"

He grimaced. "All I've got is a cold, Keezia Lorraine. Compared to what Jackson's probably goin' through—"

CLANG! CLANG! CLANG!

Fridge broke off as an alarm bell started to ring on the other end of the line. A moment later, he heard the sound of a dispatcher's voice coming through the station's P.A. system. Sick as he was, his body still snapped to alert. His pulse kicked into gear and a surge of adrenaline flooded his system. He strained to make out the information the dispatcher was announcing, but failed.

"Gotta go," Keezia said, raising her voice.

He experienced a brief flash of fear, understanding all too well what kind of situation the noisy summons might signify. He wondered fleetingly whether it would be easier to end this conversation if he didn't. Civilians had an intellectual comprehension of how dangerous firefighting could be. The men and very limited number of women who did the job knew the life-and-death truth in their gut.

"Watch out for yourself, sugar," he urged. There was a tightness in his chest that had nothing to do with his cold.

The woman Ralph Booker Randall loved and wanted to make his wife broke the connection. Whether she'd heard his admonition, which he'd uttered as much for his own sake as hers, he didn't know.

Fridge called Jackson's phone number a bunch of times during the next hour or so. All he got was a recorded message on an answering machine. He wondered briefly why Lauralee didn't pick up, then remembered that the teenager had gone out of town at the beginning of August to visit her maternal grandparents.

It was probably just as well she wasn't home, he decided. He'd always had a sense that Jackson's bright-eyed daughter harbored some unspoken anxieties about the work her daddy did. And if Jackson was as upset as Keezia had suggested...

Lauralee shouldn't have to contend with that kind of heartache.

He spent nearly a minute debating whether he should get up, get dressed and try to track down Jackson himself. Common sense forced him to abandon the notion. Given the various and sundry medications he'd taken, he wasn't sure he'd be safe behind the wheel. Just last week he'd heard some EMTs talking about an accident involving a driver who'd been doped up on cold pills and drowsed off while traveling on I-85. Not only had the man run his own vehicle into an embankment; he'd also plowed into a minivan carrying a family of five.

Eventually his thoughts settled on the red-haired psychiatrist he'd gotten to know a little more than two weeks ago at the Show and Muster. He'd told Keezia the truth when he'd said that he thought that Phoebe Donovan had something going with Jackson Miller only he doubted either one of them was sure exactly what it was. He still held to that opinion.

Nonetheless...

He dialed 411.

"Bell South," a mechanically mellifluous female voice said. "What city?"

Fridge cleared his throat. It felt as though someone had taken a cheese grater to the inside of it. "Atlanta."

"What name, please?"

"Donovan. That's *D*-as-in-dog, *O-N-O-V*-as-in-Victor, *A-N*. First name, Phoebe. Address is—" he reeled it off.

"Please wait."

He did. He also coughed a few times. He blotted his nose, then chucked the tissues he'd used into the wastebasket by the bed. He figured he'd probably used up a tree's worth of paper in the past couple days.

There were a couple of *click-click-clicks* on the other end of the line.

"Thank you for waiting," a voice said with inhumanly perfect diction. "The number is—"

Fridge listened, disconnected, then tapped in the seven-digit sequence he'd been given.

B-b-rring.

No answer.

B-b-rring.

Again, nothing. *C'mon, Phoebe,* Fridge thought, his knuckles tightening on the phone. He glanced at the bedside clock. It was two minutes past nine. He wondered whether Jackson's tenant was the type who slept in on weekends.

Someone picked up.

"H'lo."

It was more of a croak than a word. Fridge didn't recognize the voice. He wasn't even certain of its gender. Had he dialed the wrong number? he wondered. Or did Phoebe Donovan have something going with somebody other than—

"Hello?"

Okay. The voice belonged to a female. And it held a slight hint of a Bostonian accent.

"Phoebe?" Fridge asked.

There was a fractional pause. Then, suspiciously, "Who is this, please?"

She obviously didn't recognize his voice, either. Fridge could hardly blame her. Even to his own ears, he sounded like some kind of heavy-breathing phone harasser.

"It's Fridge Randall."

"*Fridge?*" There was surprise—and a sliver of fear—in Phoebe's invocation of his name. "You sound awful!"

"Got some kind of—" he paused, turning his head away from the mouthpiece and coughing "—cold bug."

"Oh." Some of the tension went out of her tone. "I'm sorry to hear that. There's a virus going around the hospital, too."

"Yeah, well, it could be worse." He coughed again. "Look, Phoebe. Why I'm calling... Does Jackson happen to be there?"

He heard a sharp intake of breath on the other end of the line and knew that his question had embarrassed her. While he regretted this, his concern about Jackson took precedence. The more he'd thought about Keezia's description of his friend, the more uneasy he'd become.

"You mean...here? With me?"

"Yeah."

"No. Jackson isn't here. Why would you—?"

He didn't let her finish the question. He didn't answer it, either. "Do you know whether he's gotten home from work yet?"

There was a pause.

"No, I don't," Phoebe replied after a moment or two. "Is something wrong?"

There was a wealth of worry in the question. It told Fridge a lot about her feelings for Jackson. It also made him feel that he'd done the right thing in calling.

"I'm—" he coughed again, his anger at his illness spiking "—not sure. The station caught an alarm on an apartment fire early this morning. There was a casualty. A little girl. Jackson found her and brought her out. There wasn't a mark on her, from what I hear. But she was stone-cold gone. Smoke inhalation, probably. That's what kills most folks in a fire, not the flames."

"Oh, dear God." It was a horrified whisper.

"Keezia got called to fill in at the station today. Seems about half the department's out sick. Anyway, she phoned me with the story. Said Jackson looked pretty shaken when she saw him at the shift change. The captain on duty mentioned somethin' about having' him talk with one of the department counselors. Jackson told him no way and drove off. I thought maybe he would stop by my place but, well…"

Fridge let the sentence trail off, feeling very unsettled.

"Have you tried to reach him?" Phoebe wanted to know.

He grimaced. "I've been callin' his number every fifteen minutes or so since seven-thirty. All I get is an answerin' machine tellin' me to leave a message." He sneezed violently, then drew a snuffling breath. His long simmering dislike of answering machines suddenly boiled over. "Man, I hate those things!"

"What about his mother?"

Fridge hesitated. He'd only met Louisa Miller a couple of times. While she'd been perfectly polite to him, there'd been a coolness about her that had rubbed him the wrong way. His first thought had been that she had a problem dealing with African-Americans. Then he'd noticed that she'd taken a standoffish attitude toward her son, too. He'd gotten the definite impression that she wasn't too pleased with Jackson's choice of careers.

"Fridge?" Phoebe pressed, apparently picking up on his reluctance to respond to her question.

"I don't believe Jackson would go to his mama with somethin' like this, Phoebe," he finally responded, choosing his words with care.

There was a long silence on the other end of the line. Fridge waited patiently, sensing that his answer had stirred some kind of inner turmoil. He wondered if Phoebe was disturbed by the implications of his assumption that Jackson would turn to her in this time of trouble rather than to a blood relative.

"Fridge?" she eventually asked.

"Still—" he tried and failed to stifle a cough "—here."

"I don't see Jackson's truck. He always parks it in the driveway when he comes home from the station."

Fridge glanced at the bedside clock, his concern about his friend increasing. "Oh, man."

"Fridge, you don't think—" She stopped abruptly, but there was no mistaking the direction her inquiry had been going.

"I don't know what to think," he told her honestly. "Maybe...maybe Jackson's out drivin' around, tryin' to clear his head. Maybe he stopped someplace to get some breakfast. Or maybe he went to church. That's what I'd do." Fridge gave a wheezy sigh, praying that Jackson had already found—or would soon find—a source of solace for the pain he must be feeling. "He's bound to come home sooner or later. And when he does, will you give me a call? My number is—"

"Hold on." He could visualize her searching for a pencil and paper. After a moment she said, "Okay. Go ahead."

He reeled off his number, punctuating the seven-digit sequence with a trio of increasingly powerful sneezes.

"Have you been to a doctor?" Phoebe questioned sharply.

"Yeah." He paused to blow his nose. "The man's got me poppin' antibiotics. And Keezia's made me a couple gallons of her mama's chicken soup. If the pills don't cure me, you can bet her home cookin' will." The herbal tea excepted, of course, he amended silently.

"Well, please, take care of yourself." The request sounded heartfelt, not pro forma. It was followed by a few moments of silence. Then, awkwardly, "Fridge, if you...if you should hear from Jackson..."

"I'll let you know, Phoebe."

Ralph Randall did hear from Jackson Miller many hours later, but there was no reason for him to inform Phoebe of the fact. That's because Jackson indicated that he was phoning from his red-haired tenant's side of his two-family house.

Precisely what had occurred between Phoebe and Jackson, Fridge never learned. Nor would it have been "mannerly" for him to ask. But something in Jackson's voice told him that his friend had gone to the right place—*the right person*—to find the comfort he'd undoubtedly needed.

Nine

Phoebe Donovan's mouth did not drop open. She didn't allow her eggplant parmigiana-laden fork to drop from her fingers with a splat, either. Still, Keezia could tell that the willowy redhead had been surprised by the information she'd just imparted. Stunned, even.

"Fridge has asked you to marry him?" Jackson Miller's tenant asked, carefully lowering her eating utensil to her plate. Her tone was as controlled as her movements.

"Uh-huh." Keezia took a chunk of crusty Italian bread from the wicker basket positioned between them. She broke it into several pieces and began using the smallest one to soak up the residue of spicy marinara sauce remaining on her plate. "Three times."

The first time had been the morning after she and Ralph Booker Randall first made love.

"It's not goin' to go away, Keezia," he'd whispered on that fateful morning she'd woken up in his arms for the first time. *"I'll keep on bein' your friend and your lover. Only that's not my bottom line. I want to be your husband. I want to be a*

daddy to the children you said you wanted to have. But if you need more time..."

The second time had been the evening of the Show and Muster, also after a passionate bout of lovemaking. She'd been cuddling contentedly against Fridge when he'd suddenly harkened back to her earlier comments about the negative reactions she frequently elicited from other firefighters' wives and girlfriends. He'd observed—lightly, but with a take-me-seriously edge—that she might go a long way toward defusing questions about her motivations and morality if she consented to become Mrs. Ralph Randall.

The third time had been that very morning, before he'd gone off to work.

"I just wanted to make certain you understand the offer's still open, Keezia Lorraine," he'd quietly declared, holding her eyes with a steady, serious gaze.

Although he'd punctuated the remark with a quick but tender kiss, something about it had made her uneasy. Had Fridge been putting her on notice that he'd finally set a limit on the amount of time he was willing to give her to consider his proposal? Had he wanted her to realize that there'd come a moment—possibly in the very near future—when his offer of marriage would be...closed?

"And you turned him down?" Phoebe questioned.

Keezia started, returning to the present. She nodded quickly, then popped the sauce-soaked morsel of bread she was holding into her mouth. After chewing and swallowing the tasty tidbit she asked, "Aren't you going to tell me I'm out of my mind?"

The counter-query came out sounding much more defensive than she'd intended. It was too much to hope that Phoebe wouldn't pick up on the tone. The woman was a trained psychiatrist, after all!

"Why should I tell you that, Keezia?" The question was cool and calm.

"Why shouldn't you?" Keezia grimaced. "Everybody else I know has."

"Well, don't go adding me to the list of those questioning your sanity just yet."

The woman Fridge Randall wanted to marry cocked her head to one side, studying Jackson Miller's tenant. Then, slowly, she started to smile. The curving of her lips felt a little lopsided, but the emotion it reflected was genuine.

She recalled the unexpected sense of affinity she'd experienced toward this white woman at the Show and Muster. That feeling had intensified during the two weeks since that initial encounter. She'd run into Phoebe on several different occasions and had very interesting conversations with her each time. They'd even shared a night out with Fridge and Jackson the previous Sunday. Nothing fancy, but lots of fun. So much so, they'd discussed doing it again before Lauralee's return from out of state.

It was still too early to say for certain, but Keezia definitely believed that Dr. Donovan and she were on the way to becoming good friends. The notion pleased her for a great many reasons.

"*That's* a relief to hear," she said wryly, referring to Phoebe's caution against including her among those who thought she might be nuts. "Having ordinary folks call me crazy is one thing. Having it come from a bona fide psychiatrist…"

There was a pause in their conversation. Phoebe finished the remainder of her entrée. Her expression seemed abstracted at first, then turned decidedly speculative.

"You're starting to wonder," Keezia accused, not really blaming the other woman. She'd been wondering about herself, too. What was it that kept her from agreeing to marry the man to whom she knew she'd given her heart?

"Wonder?" Phoebe echoed, blinking.

"About whether my saying no to Fridge might mean I'm a taco shy of a combination plate." Actually, she hadn't officially said no, *N-O*. But the result was the same as if she had.

"No," the woman across the table disputed with a lilting laugh. "I'm not."

Keezia cocked her head again, finding herself curiously unwilling to let the matter drop. She'd spent some time in counseling after she'd left Tyrell and found the experience helpful.

Maybe she could avail herself of a little of Phoebe's professional expertise as she tried to sort through her present psychological dilemma.

"But you *are* trying to figure out why I'd refuse his proposal," she asserted.

Phoebe fingered her wineglass for a second or two, then lifted it to her lips and took a drink. Eventually she said, "It's obvious Fridge means a great deal to you."

Keezia drew herself up in her seat. Emotion welled within her. It took her several moments to find her voice. Once she did, the words were no problem. They came directly from her heart.

"Ralph Randall is the best man I've ever known."

"But you don't want to marry him." The caveat was gentle and nonjudgmental.

There was a tense silence. Keezia slumped a little, weighed down by the truth she couldn't adequately explain to herself or anybody else.

"No," she agreed tightly, the single syllable bitter on her tongue. "I don't."

That Phoebe wanted to explore the reasons for this reply was obvious. But she held back, staying silent.

Keezia dropped her gaze. Expelling a heavy sigh, she began fiddling with the stem of her wineglass. She appreciated the other woman's respect for her privacy. She really did. And yet...

She needed to talk with someone. She needed it badly.

"If I married anybody, it'd be Fridge," she finally said. "It's just that..." She sighed again and fiddled with the wineglass a bit more. Eventually she raised her eyes to Phoebe. "You know I'm divorced, right?"

"You mentioned something about it last weekend."

So she had, Keezia recalled, sighing for a third time. The "something" she'd mentioned hadn't been much. A passing comment in the ladies' room, basically, offered in response to Phoebe's revelation that she'd been engaged to a man who'd died in a plane crash less than a week before their wedding date.

"The thing is," she began, her stomach knotting. "My marriage got pretty ugly before I finally found the guts to get out Tyrell—that was my husband's name, Tyrell Babcock—knocked me around. He knocked me around...a lot."

Phoebe leaned forward, compassion vivid on her fair-skinned face. "Oh, Keezia."

"I bought into everything Tyrell laid on me for nearly three years," Keezia continued doggedly, determined to disclose the facts. "Including the idea that his beating me was my fault. Then one morning I looked into the bathroom mirror and saw a woman I didn't recognize. She had a black eye and a split lip and she was wearing the kind of expression you usually see in zombie movies. After a few seconds, I realized that this woman—this *stranger*—was me." She paused, the remembered horror of that realization threatening to close her throat. She swallowed hard, then continued. "And, well, I'm not certain how to explain what happened next. But all of a sudden this little voice inside me started saying, 'This isn't right, girl. You haven't done anything to deserve this. Even if you're as worthless as Tyrell keeps telling you, which you know in your soul you aren't, you *do not* deserve to be treated this way.'"

"And you walked out?"

Keezia nodded. "I packed my things and went home to my mother. Tyrell came after me and tried to cause trouble, but I called the police on him and pressed charges. Then I got a lawyer and filed for divorce. I joined one of those support groups for battered women, too. Six months later, Tyrell was serving time for assault and I was freer than I'd been in a long, long time."

Her ex-husband was still behind bars. Her mother had phoned earlier in the week to say she'd heard from a friend back in Detroit that Tyrell had involved himself in some serious trouble in prison and been sentenced to serve at least five more years. There was also word—which her mother had passed on with audible reluctance—that he'd recently traded wedding vows with a woman he'd messed around with while still married to Keezia.

"That's remarkable." The statement was simple, sincere and full of admiration.

Keezia shrugged, knowing that she'd done very little to merit the other woman's approbation. She had no doubt that had Phoebe Donovan been in her place, she would have walked out the first time Tyrell Babcock had raised his hand to her.

"What's remarkable is that in the three years since I showed up on her doorstep, my mother's never said, 'I told you so, Keezia Lorraine.' Lord knows, she's had every right to. She warned me Tyrell Babcock was bad news from the get-go. But she's never reminded me of that. Not once." Keezia made a face, recalling some of the other things Eloise Baxter had had to say when she'd telephoned. "Of course, she *is* leading the chorus of folks who're telling me I'm nuts for not marrying Fridge."

"It takes a long time to recover from the kind of experience you went through, Keezia," Phoebe declared, her tone acquiring a hint of therapeutic soothing. "And you're the only one who can gauge how that recovery process is going. If you don't think you're ready to make a commitment—"

"There are times when I want to marry him," Keezia blurted out, the admission escaping from her in a rush. "But then I get scared. Really, truly scared. I know with my head and my heart that Fridge is nothing—*nothing!*—like Tyrell. Still, I can't help thinking that if I was a fool for love once, I might be a fool for love again."

Phoebe frowned, her normally smooth forehead wrinkling like a piece of corrugated cardboard. Her question, when it came, was blunt. "Are you afraid Fridge might abuse you?"

"No!" Keezia shook her head in vehement denial, wishing there was a more potent word to use. "Oh, Lord, no. He's never even raised his *voice* to me." The closest he'd come had been when he'd angrily informed her that he hadn't kept company with her for three long years because he wanted to get into her panties. But he'd apologized for his tone and choice of words within seconds. "It's just that...that...oh, I don't know how to explain it, Phoebe!" Would that she did.

"Maybe I could get over whatever it is that's messing me up if he wasn't so damned big. Because every once in a while, I flash on what it would be like if a man of his size laid into me the way Tyrell did."

It had happened just the other afternoon, in fact. They'd been working on one of the many community betterment projects in which Helen Rose Randall took a personal interest. In this particular instance, the construction of a playground on a small plot of donated land.

Keezia had found herself watching Fridge, noting how easily he performed the hard labor required of him. He'd lugged lumber. Unloaded and stacked iron bars. Handled bags of gravel as though they were stuffed with foam pellets instead of stones.

She'd relished the display of his physical prowess, especially after he'd decided to discard his shirt. The sight of his powerful muscles rippling beneath his dark, sweat-sheened skin had stirred her feminine juices and sparked her capacity for sexual fantasizing.

But then something had happened. Her imagination had turned against her. Her lover's size had been transformed into a source of intimidation. His strength into—

"Have you talked about this with Fridge?" Phoebe wanted to know.

Keezia nodded jerkily, wishing she could shove the memory of what had occurred aside. Fridge, as he so often did, had sensed her atavistic reaction to him. He'd done what he could to reassure her, but they'd both known that she was the only one who could exorcise the demons from her past.

"He's been so sweet," she said. "But I know it hurts him. Knowing I get frightened of him sometimes, I mean. And that makes *me* hurt."

Their waiter—a young man who'd introduced himself earlier as Mario—chose that particular moment to appear at their table.

"May I get you ladies some dessert?" he queried as he began clearing their plates.

"Ah, no," Phoebe said after a moment. "Thank you."

"I'm fine, too," Keezia replied, reacting to the interruption with a combination of relief and regret. She and Phoebe had been getting in a little deep.

"Cappuccino?" Mario coaxed. "Espresso?"

Keezia saw Phoebe check her watch. She did the same, noting that it was a few minutes past eight. They'd have to get themselves in gear if they were going to make the eight-thirty showing of the movie they were planning to see.

"None for me," she told Mario, then glanced across the table. "Phoebe?"

"None for me, either," came the crisp response. "If we could get our check, please?"

"Sure." The waiter nodded amiably. "I'll be back with that in just a minute."

"So, what about you?" Keezia asked as Mario bustled off. Although she knew from past visits that the service in the midtown restaurant in which they were eating was good, she also realized that the 'just a minute' line was an exaggeration. She figured she had a time for a little quid pro quo.

"Me?" Phoebe dabbed at her mouth with her napkin.

"You and Jackson." Keezia eyed the other woman curiously. Although he was too gentlemanly to cite specifics, Fridge had indicated that Jackson's relationship with Phoebe had come to some kind of turning point the morning after the death of baby Anne. "I'm done pouring out my heart for the evening. It's your turn to give."

Phoebe said nothing for ten or fifteen seconds, the look on her fine-boned face difficult to read. Then, very slowly, she conceded, "I'm not certain what to say, Keezia."

"I'm not asking for X-rated details." She kept her tone light, acting as though it was no big deal. She thought about some of the things she'd observed at the concert they'd attended the previous Sunday night. The casual touching. The easy exchange of glances. Nothing overt or embarrassing, but definitely signaling the existence of an intimate bond. "Even though it's obvious to anyone with any sense that you and Jackson have been doing the nasty."

She wasn't certain what kind of reaction she expected this

statement to evoke. What she got was an intensely satisfied, uniquely female smile.

"Actually," Phoebe began in a butter-wouldn't-melt-in-her-mouth tone, "what Jackson and I have been doing has been very nice."

Keezia gave a knowing laugh. "Girl," she returned, infusing some street sass into her voice. "If the look on your lily-white face is anything to go by, it's been a lot better than *that!*"

"Mmm…"

"Are you two getting serious?"

The question plainly caught Phoebe by surprise. The smile faded from her face. She flushed slightly and averted her gaze.

Keezia let a few seconds tick by, debating whether to press the issue. She finally decided to try a small nudge. If it didn't work, she would back off.

"Phoebe?"

The redhead looked at her. "I…I don't know."

"You don't know about you? Or you don't know about him?"

"I don't know about either of us."

Keezia frowned, remembering Fridge's initial assessment of the relationship between Jackson and Phoebe. After a moment she asked what seemed like the obvious question.

"You care about Jackson, don't you?"

The extra color that had risen in Phoebe's cheeks abruptly receded. She nodded, the movement of her head a little stiff.

"And he cares about you."

"I suppose."

"You *suppose?*" That didn't square with what she'd seen at the concert. Nor with anything she'd heard about Jackson Miller. The man had a reputation for making his priorities—and his commitments—very clear.

"He's never said anything, Keezia."

Keezia raised her eyebrows. "It's not what a man says, Phoebe. It's what he does."

"Fridge has told you how he feels, hasn't he?"

"That's different." The answer was immediate and unequivocal. Inexplicable, too. Still, it *was* different. "But don't go trying to change the subject on me. We're talking about *you.*"

There was a pause. Something that looked a lot like guilt flickered through Phoebe's green-gold eyes.

"Jackson tells me I do that a lot," she finally observed.

"What?"

"Try to shift conversations off me and onto somebody else."

"Do you?"

Phoebe sighed. "Yes," she admitted frankly. "I never realized it until Jackson called me on it. But yes, I do."

"It's usually the other way around. Most people try to shift the subject off others and onto themselves."

"I guess I'm not 'most people.'"

"I don't think Jackson would be interested in you if you were."

The redhead leaned forward. "Has he said something to you, Keezia?"

Keezia hesitated, surprised by the other woman's need for reassurance. She'd pegged Phoebe Donovan as someone with a very high level of self-esteem.

"Not the way you mean, no," she finally replied. "But I've got eyes, Phoebe. I've seen the two of you together."

"Has he said something to Fridge?"

"About you?"

"Yes."

"Probably." It was as definite an answer as she could offer.

"You don't *know?*" The astonishment in Phoebe's question revealed volumes about her perception of Keezia's relationship with Fridge.

"No," Keezia said, wondering how she could explain the situation. She decided to tell the flat-out truth. "And I wouldn't try to find out, either. Fridge and Jackson have been working side by side for nearly ten years. They couldn't get any tighter if you glued them together. What they talk about when I'm not around…"

* * *

"Do you think they're talkin' about us tonight?"

"Who? Phoebe and Keezia?"

Fridge silently reordered the names to suit his personal priorities. "Yeah."

"Probably. What do you think?"

"There isn't a doubt in my mind."

The time was a few minutes before 10:00 p.m. on what had been an unusually quiet Sunday. While most of the other members of the A shift had hit their bunks, Fridge and Jackson had decided to sit outside and talk a bit.

Fridge appreciated the down time. He truly did. But he also chafed at the lack of action. It almost made him wish for a repeat of the ridiculous incident that had enlivened his last twenty-four-hour stint at the station.

It had happened around noon. A woman had driven up onto the station's front lawn, then come staggering out of her car clutching the back of her skull and shrieking something about having been shot in the head. She'd taken two steps, stumbled and fallen to the ground.

He'd reached her first, with Jackson barely a stride behind. Working as a team, they'd managed to control the hysterical woman and get her hands away from her alleged wound.

There'd been no blood. No...brains.

What there *had* been was a white mushy blob of something smeared into the woman's bleached, stiffly sprayed hair.

Fridge had taken a cautious sniff of the stuff and immediately thought of the fresh bread his mother often baked for Sunday supper.

"Dough?" he'd asked dubiously.

Jackson's mouth twitched. "Poppin' fresh, I think."

Indeed. It had turned out that the woman had been grocery shopping. But instead of going directly home with her purchases—including a fresh-from-the-dairy-case cylinder of crescent rolls clearly marked Keep Refrigerated—she'd driven around doing errands. Which might have been all right had her car's air-conditioning not been on the fritz. The sweltering August sun had turned the interior of the vehicle into...well, basically, an oven. The baking rolls had risen to a certain point, then blown the cylinder apart.

"How's it going with you and Keezia?" Jackson asked, breaking what had been a fairly lengthy silence.

Fridge emptied his lungs in a gusty sigh. "Same old, same old. She's still dealin' with what that bastard she was married to did to her. God, I hate that son of a bitch! I know it isn't Christian, but I really do."

It wasn't Christian to wish another human being dead or beaten to a bloody pulp, either, but he'd been doing that, too.

Jackson nodded. "Tyrell Babcock will get his one of these days. As for Keezia—she's got a lot to get behind her, man. Give her time."

"Oh, I intend to, Jackson." Fridge paused, an all-too-familiar feeling of frustration welling up within him. "I just wish she'd let me help her more, you know?"

"Hey. She's an independent woman."

Fridge gave a rumbling laugh, his mood lightening a bit. "You've got that right." And if truth be told, he wouldn't have had it any other way.

There was another silence. Fridge shifted his position and stretched his legs out in front of him.

"Speakin' of independent women," he picked up. "How're things with you and Phoebe?"

Jackson moved around a little. "Good question."

"Got any good answers?"

"Not yet."

"Uh-huh." Fridge smoothed his mustache. "You still tryin' to understand her?"

"I'm doing my best."

Fridge shifted his position again. "I've said it before and I'll say it again. If the good Lord had meant for men to understand women, He would have put the explanation in writing."

"You seem to understand Keezia pretty well."

"Oh, I understand her just fine when she's on the job, actin' like a firefighter. But the rest of the time? Give me a break. I feel like I'm stumblin' around in a minefield at midnight."

Jackson sighed. "I hear you."

Yet another silence.

"You're goin' to have to make some kind of decision pretty soon, Jackson," Fridge finally felt compelled to point out. He knew he was marching into touchy territory, but he couldn't keep silent. "Unless you're plannin' to keep carryin' on with Phoebe after Lauralee comes home from Baltimore?"

Jackson stiffened visibly. "What kind of question is that, Fridge?" he demanded, turning in his chair. "God Almighty! 'Carrying on'? I have a relationship with Phoebe the same way you have a relationship with Keezia!"

"I don't think so," Fridge countered, refusing to back away from the point he was trying to make. "'Cuz in *my* relationship, I've asked the lady to marry me."

Not that it had done him much good, he reflected. But he'd put it on the record. Repeatedly. He wanted Keezia Lorraine Carew to be his bride, not just his bedmate.

He glanced over at his friend, knowing he'd pushed a little too hard. He felt the need to make amends.

"Hey, Jackson?"

Jackson turned his head. "Yeah?"

"I didn't mean to rile you, brother."

"Sure you did." The retort was quick, reasserting the bantering rhythm of a long and deep friendship.

"Well, maybe just a little," Fridge conceded, chuckling. "But it was for your own good."

"Uh-huh. And I'm sure it hurt you much more than it hurt me."

"Oh, definitely."

A few moments slipped by. Then Jackson breathed out on a long, slow sigh. "You're right, you know."

"About what?" As if he really needed to ask.

"I *do* have to make a decision about Phoebe."

Amen to that, Fridge thought.

An instant later, the station's alarm bell began to clang.

It was right around 11 p.m. and Keezia and Phoebe were seated at a small table in a café in the upscale and very social section of Atlanta known as Buckhead. The place was bustling. One of the main attractions seemed to be a big-screen color television bracketed to the wall behind the long, polished wood bar.

"Do you know what I truly loved about that movie?" Keezia inquired, darting a quick glance at the TV screen. It was just about time for the late local news.

"The fact that the lead actor took off all his clothes—twice?" Phoebe guessed through a mouthful of key lime pie.

Keezia laughed, thinking again how much she liked the red-head's company. "Besides that."

Phoebe took a moment to swallow. "Frankly," she said, "I thought the whole thing was great. It was terrific to see a film about a woman who succeeds without behaving like a bitch or a bimbo."

"Exactly!" A nod underscored her agreement. "And she didn't have to blow anybody away in the process, either. Not that I think she wouldn't have been able to. I mean, that lady was one tough cop."

"*Very* tough."

Keezia took another bite of her cherry cheesecake, savoring the tart-sweet tang of the fruit and the creamy richness of the filling. Once she cleared her mouth she commented, "I thought about joining the police department."

"Really?"

"Uh-huh. I took the entrance exam for it the same month I took the one for the fire department. Passed both of 'em, too."

"What made you choose firefighting?"

"Lots of different things. Public image, for one."

"Public image?" Phoebe seemed surprised.

Keezia ate another mouthful of cheesecake before trying to explain. "Folks genuinely like firefighters. They see one coming, they feel good. Firefighters do things like rescuing people and saving property. But folks see a cop and they figure somebody's going to get in trouble. Even if that somebody isn't them, it triggers negative associations. I mean, have you ever heard of firefighter brutality? Or of some innocent bystander getting hosed down by accident?''

"I get your point."

"I'll also admit I liked the idea of helping break down some stereotypes about what women supposedly can and can't do." More than liked it, actually. Loved it. Succeeding as a female firefighter had been crucial to rebuilding her shattered self-esteem.

Phoebe nodded as though she understood the feelings that had shaped Keezia's career choice. After a moment she asked, "How many women firefighters are there in Atlanta?"

"Less than two dozen, last time I checked. There were only fourteen when I joined."

"That's not very many."

"Especially not when you consider there's about nine hundred active firefighters in the department."

Phoebe speared another bite of pie. "Where do you see your career going?"

"I'm still working on that," Keezia admitted, because she was. "I know I want to do more than haul hose between now and retirement. I'm ambitious. I want to move up in rank, take on more responsibility."

"Is it difficult to get promoted? Jackson's been in the department for fourteen years and he's only a lieutenant."

Keezia couldn't help laughing. "Phoebe, there are lieutenants and there are *lieutenants*. Jackson Miller could make captain like—" she snapped her fingers "—if he decided to. I know for a fact that the top brass keeps talking to him about taking a slot at the training academy." Fridge had been approached, too. "He could do a lot of good there, teaching what he knows. Jackson has a *gift* for firefighting. Maybe it's in his genes. Or maybe he takes the job more personally than a lot of us because of what happened to his father. But he's about the best in the department and everybody knows it."

"He loves his work."

Keezia tilted her head, wondering about the edge she heard. "Is that a problem for you?"

Phoebe sustained her questioning gaze for several moments,

then looked down at the table. "What he does scares me," she confessed in a tight voice. "I don't want to…I mean, the possibility that something might happen—"

About midway through this admission, Keezia registered that there was a fire showing on the big-screen TV. She focused on the incendiary image with a mixture of concern and curiosity. After a second or two of scrutiny, those emotions metastasized into something close to terror.

"Oh, dear God," she whispered, her breath jamming in her throat.

Phoebe's head came up with a jerk.

"Turn it up!" Keezia called, stumbling to her feet. She was trembling. Fear fisted, cold and greasy, in the pit of her stomach.

Heads swung in their direction. The audio from the television remained low.

"Dammit! Turn the sound up!"

"…out of control," the set suddenly blared. "Three firefighters are confirmed dead. At least two others have been seriously injured—"

"Keezia—?"

"I know the building," Keezia Lorraine Carew said starkly. "It's a construction company warehouse and it's in our zone. Fridge and Jackson are at that fire."

Keezia drove them to the site, pushing her junker to the limits of its capabilities all the way. Phoebe had offered her car, but it had been plain that she was in no condition to drive it. After briefly considering taking the wheel of the redhead's vehicle, Keezia had decided that it was wiser to stick with the automobile she knew.

Within a few seconds of arriving on the scene, she realized that things were bad. Very, very bad. She searched frantically for a familiar face, praying that she would see Fridge or Jackson or both. She finally spotted her old mentor, Sam Fields. He was bent over by the side of a pumper truck, retching.

The news he imparted when he stopped heaving up the remains of his Sunday supper made her want to vomit, too.

Three firefighters lost. Among them, a probie named Daniels whom Phoebe apparently had met and Mitch Jones.

"M-Mitch?" Keezia echoed, horrified. It wasn't possible! "But how, Sam? He wasn't even supposed to be on duty!"

"Bucking for some overtime, I guess."

Oh, God. Oh…God.

Jackson was all right as far as Sam knew. But Fridge…

"He was hurt, Keez," was the grim bottom line. "Bad. Burns. Broken bones. Probably some internal injuries. Goddamned barrel of illegally stored solvent blew up and brought down a piece of the ceiling. Jackson dragged him out somehow. They put him in an ambulance and took him away."

"He's alive?" Keezia was desperate. "You're sure?"

Sam gave a hacking cough. Mucus—the legacy of the so-called "snotty" smoke being generated by this blaze—streamed from his nostrils. He wiped it away with the back of one hand.

"He was breathin' when they put him in the ambulance, Keezia," he answered hoarsely. "That's all I know."

It was all anyone knew for many anguished hours. Keezia kept vigil at the hospital with Helen Rose Randall, her heart leaping into her throat every time a doctor or a nurse approached them.

"I thank you again for calling me, Keezia," Fridge's mother murmured, patting her hand.

"You needed to be here," was all Keezia could think of to say. She was deeply grateful for the other woman's presence. Helen Rose Randall was much smaller and slighter than her son, but she shared his moral strength. The woman was a rock.

Willie Leroy Randall's widow was a rotund woman of great dignity and warmth. Her hair was pure silver, her complexion the color of bittersweet chocolate. She was impeccably groomed.

"I remember…back when Ralph was just a little boy. No more than six. He saw an illustration of hell in one of his Sunday-school books."

Keezia blinked at this sudden detour down Memory Lane. "W-what?"

"A picture of hell. The burning pit. Scared him half to death, I think. He told me the flames seemed like they were out to get him...personally."

"Oh." Keezia could barely control a shudder.

"I sometimes wonder if that picture didn't start him on the path to becoming a firefighter," Helen Rose Randall mused, continuing to stroke Keezia's hand. "He's always been one for facing down fears."

"I—"

Keezia broke off as an exhausted-looking white man in stained surgical scrubs appeared. "Miz Randall?" he asked.

"Yes, sir," Fridge's mother replied, squeezing Keezia's fingers.

The doctor knuckled his red-rimmed eyes, then swiftly summarized Fridge's injuries and the surgical procedures he'd undergone since arriving at the hospital. While his condition remained critical, there was reason for hope.

"The next twenty-four hours will be crucial," the man concluded, his compassionate gaze moving from Helen Rose to Keezia and back again. "But he's a real fighter. I could tell that on the table. And when a patient won't give up, well, let's just say the human spirit can be as important as medical science in this kind of case."

"My boy's a survivor," Fridge's mother declared. Her voice was steady, the expression on her seamed face serene.

"Fridge is strong," Keezia agreed, close to tears. He was alive. The man she loved was alive! "And we're going to be with him every step of the way."

Ten

Fridge lost most of the week immediately following the fire. Oh, there were a few things that made lasting impressions. Lifting his swollen eyelids and catching a drug-blurred glimpse of Keezia's anxiety-ravaged yet beautiful face, for one. Hearing his mama praying for his recovery in a soft, steady voice, for another. Being driven to the screaming point and beyond during an excruciating process in which medical personnel scrubbed off his burnt skin in preparation for a grafting operation, for a third. But for the most part—the merciful most part, in many ways—the period was a blank.

He surfaced into something close to lucidity shortly before dawn on the seventh day of his ordeal. It took him nearly a minute to sort out where he was and how he'd gotten there. Assessing his condition required even more time. There were tubes sprouting from several parts of his body and a cast encasing his right foot. His right arm, hand and thigh were wrapped, mummy-style, and his chest and shoulders were bandaged with gauze and tape. Some sort of supportive collar surrounded his neck and rubbed annoyingly beneath his chin.

He was in pain. A lot of it. But bad as it was, it seemed curiously secondhand—as though there were some kind of filter between the hurt and his experiencing of it.

Medication, he decided. They'd probably doped him to the gills. With what, he had no clue. However, he did vaguely recall having heard a fellow firefighter talk about what it had been like to be dosed with morphine following a near-fatal accident. The drug had definitely done its job, the man had said. He'd felt no physical pain at all. Psychological pain had been a different story. According to him, the morphine had done a terrible number on his head. He claimed he'd reached a mental state in which he'd actually persuaded himself that several members of the hospital staff were conspiring to murder him.

Fridge tried to shift his position. His body issued an immediate and agonizing protest. He groaned, the fingers of his good hand spasming against the bedsheets. Cold beads of sweat popped on his forehead and upper lip. His stomach roiled.

"Fridge?" The invocation of his name held a mix of sleepiness and uncertainty.

His pulse stuttered. After a second or two he turned his head a little bit, fearing that he might be hallucinating. How could he possibly be hearing—

"F-Fridge?" The sleepiness was gone. The uncertainty had acquired an edge of please-don't-let-me-be-dreaming desperation.

Suddenly Keezia was there. There, by the side of his hospital bed. He glanced beyond her for a moment, registering the outline of what looked like a cot. There was a pile of sheets on one end and what appeared to be a mashed-down pillow on the other.

She'd been staying in his room, he realized, his heart starting to bang against his ribs. Keezia Lorraine Carew had been with him through the night, like some kind of guardian angel.

Watching over him.

Waiting for him to wake up.

Leaning over the bed's safety railing, Keezia skimmed her

fingertips lightly against his face. She seemed to be trying to verify that he was solid flesh, not some kind of phantom. After a few moments of caressing him, she reached up and switched on a small overhead light. He blinked against the flare of illumination. His vision shimmered out of focus, then snapped back in.

"Oh, Fridge," she whispered, tears coursing down her face and dripping off her chin. The lids of her eyes were puffy; the whites, badly bloodshot. There were hollows beneath her exotically angled cheekbones that he'd never seen before. She looked as though she hadn't eaten or slept in days. "Oh...*Fridge*. Thank God."

"Keez...ia." He could barely get her name out. He paused, scraping together enough breath to go on. He didn't want her to weep. The sight of her crying ripped at his gut. "Don't..."

She shushed him, pressing her fingers gently against his mouth. Then she smiled. The curving of her full lips was heartbreakingly lovely, like sunshine coming through rain.

"Don't try to talk, baby," she said huskily. "They had a tube down your throat until last night and it's probably a little raw."

"I—" Somewhere in the back of his mind he noticed that she was wearing the orange Hot Stuff T-shirt she'd appropriated from him after the Show and Muster. The garment was spotted with stains and badly rumpled.

"Shhh. Shhh." She caressed his lips again, her topaz eyes glowing like gemstones. Her fingers were trembling. "There'll be plenty of time for that later. Everything's going to be all right, Fridge. You're back with us now...and everything's going to be just fine."

Only everything wasn't.

Going to be "just fine," that is.

Fridge got his official prognosis two weeks and two days after he was admitted to the hospital. He picked the time to press his doctor for details very carefully, making certain that neither his mother nor Keezia would be present when he did so. He wanted—*needed*—to face the truth about his future by himself, on his own.

The medical verdict was cruelly simple. He would recover, eventually, but he would never, ever be as good as new. No matter how much work or will he put into the effort, a complete healing wasn't going to happen. His flesh would bear scars from the fire for the rest of his life. He would also be left with a permanently weakened back.

The bottom line: He was finished with firefighting.

Or, to put it more accurately, firefighting was finished with *him*.

Although his physician ended their meeting on an upbeat note and exited stressing the positive, all Fridge could focus on was the fact that he'd been declared unfit for the profession he loved. The profession in which he'd been among the best of the best was now closed to him. As he grappled with the question of what he might be able to do with the rest of his life, he found himself remembering something he'd told Keezia the night he'd driven her home from the retirement party and kissed her, man to woman, for the first time.

"Baby," he'd begun. *"Baby, listen to me. I'm bigger than you. That's a fact and neither one of us can change it. But don't you understand? I know what being bigger means. I know my own strength. It's been…well, it's been a gift to me. Same as my singing voice. My strength has helped me save lives, Keezia. I respect it. I don't use it against people. And I would never—ever—use it to hurt you."*

He squeezed his eyelids shut, terrified that he might start to bawl like a baby. He fought the possibility, staving off tears with every shred of self-discipline he possessed. To allow himself to weep would only underscore how great a loss he'd sustained.

He'd told the woman he loved that he respected his strength. This was true. What he hadn't told her was how much pride he'd always taken in it. He truly relished his physical power. He *liked* walking into a room and discovering that he was the biggest dude in the place. It was an integral part of the man he believed himself to be.

It was integral to Keezia's vision of him, too. Because for all that they sometimes unnerved her, he knew his size and prowess frequently turned her on. He'd seen her—*felt* her, really—checking him out a few weeks back when they'd been working on his mother's playground project. He'd strutted his stuff a bit in response to her scrutiny, stripping off his shirt and flexing his muscles more often than he really needed. He'd known that he'd had her mouth watering, and he'd started getting hot and hard because of it. Had Keezia not suddenly turned skittish and shaky on him, there was no telling what might have happened.

And now—

There was a knock on the door to his hospital room. A moment later, the door eased open and Jackson Miller stepped in.

"Hey, Fridge."

"Hey…Jackson." Fridge made a conscious effort to lighten his mood.

"Busy?"

Knowing it was expected, he managed a small, sardonic snort. "Oh, Yeah. Booked solid. Just takin' a little break from my Olympic decathlon trainin', you know? Figurin' to start workin' on my pole vaultin' in a couple minutes."

Jackson flashed a grin, then advanced into the room. There was a spring in his step Fridge had never noticed before. In noticing it now, he experienced a sudden and terrible pang of envy. Despite their differences, he'd always viewed himself as Jackson Miller's equal. He couldn't do that anymore.

Reaching the left side of the bed, Jackson made a show of looking around. "If a person didn't know better," he drawled, "he might get the impression that you're a real popular dude."

"Uh-huh." Fridge glanced briefly at the flower arrangements clustered on top of the bureau on the far side of the room. He'd dispatched the floral overflow—plus Lord knew how many bunches of balloons, plush toy animals and goodie baskets—to other parts of the hospital. But the stuff kept coming. And coming. He'd been inundated by get-well cards and letters, too. His mama had taken to taping them up on the walls. In another couple days, she'd have them completely covered. "I'm the man of the moment."

"Heard the mayor came to see you."

"My congressman, too." Fridge snorted a second time, remembering. "Just happened to have a TV camera crew with him."

"Running again, huh?"

"Runnin' always, far as I can see. Guess he figures posin' with me will win him the overcooked and crippled vote."

Jackson's lips thinned. His eyes darkened. "The doctors say—"

"They say I'm gonna mend," Fridge cut in, regretting the bitterness of his previous comment. He had no call to vent his pain on Jackson. "Gonna get up and walk again. Run, even, as long as I don't have designs on doin' a marathon. But I'm gonna be scarred like a Zulu warrior from the burns and grafts and I'm through as a firefighter." He grimaced. "Stick a fork in my career, man. It's definitely done."

Jackson studied him silently for what seemed like a long time. "I'm sorry, Fridge," he finally said, his voice tight, his spine stiff. "Truly sorry."

"Why? It's no fault of yours."

"If I'd gotten to you sooner—"

"Don't do that to yourself, man," Fridge interrupted sharply. "If you'd gotten to me later, I'd be dead. *You saved my life, Jackson.* And you risked your own when you did it. So forget the second-guessing, okay?"

There was a difficult silence. Finally Jackson dipped his head and said, "Okay."

Fridge expelled a breath he hadn't realized he'd been holding. "So, what's happenin'?" he asked after a moment "I thought I heard somethin' on the news about the owner of the warehouse bein' arrested. But with the medication they've been givin' me, I have a hard time separatin' reality from hallucinations and hopeful thinkin'."

His friend's expression hardened. "You heard right. The cops hauled the son of a bitch in yesterday. Three counts of negligent homicide and a bunch of other charges. Word is, his lawyer's looking to cut some kind of deal.''

"The D.A. gonna go for it?"

"Right after they start making ice cream in hell. I take it you didn't see that investigative report last night on—'' Jackson mentioned a local TV station.

"Can't say that I did."

"Well, our least favorite newsman decided to take a break from shoving mikes in people's faces and asking stupid questions. He did some bona fide journalistic digging. Turns out there's illegal storage at two more properties the warehouse guy owns. There's also indications he may have been paying off safety inspectors. Plus, the bastard has had trouble with the law in at least three other states." Jackson bared his teeth. His blue eyes were filled with a cold, killing rage. "I hope they fry his butt."

"Man gets convicted and sentenced to heavy time, they may be doin' worse to his butt than fryin' it."

"Yeah." There was a wealth of grim pleasure in the syllable.

"Any other news?" Fridge asked after a brief silence. For all the chitchat, his instincts told him that this was no casual call. His friend had come visiting with a purpose. But exactly what that purpose was, he couldn't tell.

"As a matter of fact, yeah. There is." Jackson paused, seeming to ponder precisely what his next words should be. Eventually he said, "I'm being reassigned, Fridge. I'm going to teach at the fire academy."

Again, Fridge experienced a terrible pang of envy. It was laced with an equally awful sense of impotence. The notion of becoming an instructor at the academy had always been in the back of his mind. And now...

"Gonna teach 'em all you know, huh?" he queried, trying to keep his tone easy and offhand. The last thing he wanted was for Jackson—for *anyone*—to sense the emotions that where whirling through him.

"Including everything I learned from you."

"Like, watch out for fallin' ceilings?"

"Fridge—"

"It's okay, man," he quickly backtracked. "I'm sincerely glad for you. You'll be a fine instructor. Only—"

"Only—what?"

"Only, the department's been offerin' you an academy slot for at least three years. Why are you takin' it now? If it has somethin' to do with my situation…" Fridge let his voice trail off.

"It's related," Jackson admitted, raking a hand back through his hair. "But not the way I think you mean. Partly because of what happened to you, Lauralee finally broke down and admitted she's scared of my job. Always has been. Only it seems my mother told her that Miller women play brave and keep their mouths shut, no matter what. Some kind of family tradition, she claimed."

"Oh, *man.*" Fridge shook his head. Louisa Miller was one cold-hearted woman, he decided with a tinge of disgust. He tried to picture a scenario in which his own mother would fob off a frightened child in such a fashion. He couldn't do it. "So you're givin' up the line for Lauralee, huh?"

Jackson's mouth quirked. "Well, my wife-to-be let me know that she's not real crazy about the idea of me running into burning buildings when everybody else is running out, either."

It took Fridge a moment to pick up on what obviously was intended to be the key phrase in his friend's statement. But once he did—

"Wife-to-be?"

"Yeah."

"Are you tellin' me that you and Phoebe—?"

Jackson didn't say a word. He simply grinned, proud as the proverbial peacock. His expression said it all.

Envy—mixed with an even more toxic emotion he couldn't put a name to—slashed at Fridge once again. He tried not to think about the conversation he and Jackson had been having when the station alarm had rung, summoning him to the fire that would lay him so desperately low.

"When?" he asked after a few moments.

"About two weeks."

"No rush, huh?"

"Well, now that we've decided..."

"I hear you." He smiled briefly. It felt awkward, but it was from the heart. "And I appreciate you comin' here to share the happy news."

"Actually, I came because I have a favor to ask."

"Of me?"

"Yeah."

"I owe you my life, Jackson. Whatever you want, it's yours."

"What I want is to have you be my best man."

Fridge's breath caught in his throat. Had he still been hooked up to a cardiac monitor, it probably would have started beeping like crazy. The nurses down the hall would have been calling Code Blue and yelling for a crash cart—*stat.*

"You...you want me to stand up with you?" he finally managed.

"Uh-huh."

"Man." Fridge ran his tongue over his suddenly dry lips, both touched and terrified by the request. "I don't—I mean—hell, Jackson! I can't even get out of bed and go to the john by myself. They've got me peeing in a pot!"

"I don't give a damn if you come to my wedding strapped to a gurney and wearing a diaper." The reply was quick and unequivocal. "You're the nearest thing to a brother I have, Fridge. I want you—*I need* you—to be with me when I say 'I do' to Phoebe."

There was only one answer a man like Ralph Booker Randall could give to such a plea.

He gave it.

Although their friendship had ripened into something very special in the days immediately following Fridge's injury, Keezia had been both surprised and moved when Phoebe Donovan asked her to be her matron of honor. She'd accepted with alacrity, eager to have a part in what promised to be a joyous occasion. But as the big moment approached, she found herself wondering whether she was up to discharging her duties.

To put it simply, she wasn't certain whether she was going to be able to get the bride to the wedding in a timely fashion.

"Phoebe?" she asked, rapping on the door to one of the stalls in the ladies' lavatory located down the hall from Fridge's hospital room. "When I said 'you go, girl' earlier, this wasn't exactly what I meant."

There was a noisy *flush* from inside the stall. Keezia moved back, crossing her fingers that the bladder crisis was finally over. A moment later, the door swung open and Phoebe stepped out, the heels of her shoes clicking against the tile floor.

"Sorry," the bride-to-be apologized with an embarrassed laugh. She paused to smooth the front of the ivory silk suit she was wearing. "I know this is the fourth—"

"Fifth."

"Fifth? Are you sure?"

"Positive." Keezia smiled teasingly as she scrutinized Phoebe from head to toe. She was more than pleased by what she saw. Peeing problems aside, the woman she was supposed to be attending could have walked out of the pages of some quietly elegant bridal magazine. "I counted. I think you may be on the verge of qualifying for some kind of world's record."

Phoebe gave another laugh, a becoming flush staining her milky-pale cheeks. She patted at her red-gold hair, which had been tamed into a sophisticated upsweep.

"Prenuptial nerves," she declared.

"Is that your professional diagnosis?" Keezia plucked a minuscule piece of lint from the left shoulder of Phoebe's trim, Chanel-style jacket, then made a delicate adjustment of the garment's right lapel. She wanted everything to be perfect for her friend.

"Well…"

Keezia cocked her head, a sudden prickle of concern skittering up her spine. She thought back to the conversation she and Phoebe had had the night of Fridge's accident. "You don't still have doubts about Jackson's feelings, do you?"

The color in Phoebe's cheeks intensified. A lambently lovely glow entered her wide, green-gold eyes. "Oh, no," she said softly. "Not anymore."

"And you're sure about *your* feelings?"

Phoebe gave her an affectionate look, followed by a quick hug. "I've never been so sure about anything in my life, Keezia," she answered. "I'm just a little keyed up, you know? And sometimes when I get keyed up—"

The door to the ladies' room swung open and Lauralee Miller poked her head in. Her flaxen hair was wreathed with flowers. She was serving as Phoebe's maid of honor.

"Y'all ready yet?" she asked anxiously, wrinkling her freckle-dusted nose. "Daddy's just about paced a hole in the floor in Fridge's room. He's gettin' *really* nervous."

The bride-to-be and her matron of honor exchanged looks, their lips twitching.

"C'mon," Keezia said, picking up her friend's delicately beribboned bouquet and handing it to her with a flourish. It amused her to note that the news of Jackson's jitters seemed to have had a very calming effect on Phoebe. "Let's go set the man's mind at ease."

The ceremony that united Phoebe Irene Donovan and Jackson Stuart Miller was short, sweet and sentimentally satisfying. Of this, Keezia was certain. But had she been asked to provide further details, she would have drawn a blank. Unlike everyone else in attendance, she spent very little time focusing on the bride and groom as they exchanged their vows. Her attention was riveted on the best man.

The ordeal of the past month had exacted a considerable toll on Fridge, she reflected. His short-cropped hair showed a faint frosting of silver in several places and there were strands of silver in his mustache as well. The lines in his face had deepened considerably. While his complexion had regained much of its natural coloration, it still had an ashy undertone.

None of these things mattered, however. As far as Keezia

Lorraine Carew was concerned, Ralph Booker Randall was the most compelling man in the room. In *any* room.

Fridge's gaze met and fused with hers a split second after Jackson enfolded Phoebe in their first embrace as husband and wife. An electric thrill sizzled through her nervous system. Her heart went into a slow, seamless swoon. Fear fell away from her soul like dead leaves taken by an autumn wind.

I love you, she thought. *With all I am, with all I have...I love you.*

Exactly when she decided how she intended to prove this love, Keezia could never pinpoint. It wasn't an all-at-once thing. She'd been moving toward the decision since the night of Fridge's accident.

Still, one fact about the timing of her making up her mind was beyond dispute. She definitely did it *before* the new Mrs. Jackson Miller took aim and tossed the bridal bouquet directly into her hands.

Keezia had to work the day after Phoebe and Jackson's wedding. Although the shift was a fairly busy one, there were no "bad" calls—no deaths, no serious injuries. For this she was deeply grateful.

Mitch Jones's loss was still acutely felt. His replacement was an experienced firefighter with an excellent reputation, but he hadn't quite found his place at the station. The crew's emotional balance was off. So, too, the rhythm of the bantering between J.T. Wilson and Bobby Robbins.

And yet...there were signs that the healing process was under way. Chief among them, that Keezia and her shift mates had stopped shying from speaking Mitch's name. Memories of him were being shared again. *Good* memories.

After clocking off at the end of her twenty-four hours, Keezia drove home to her apartment. She found Shabazz in a cranky mood, which wasn't unexpected. The cat clearly missed Fridge.

She shampooed and showered, dried off and got dressed. There was no need to debate over wardrobe choices. She'd laid out a black jacket and the snug-fitting yellow jumpsuit she'd worn to the Show and Muster *before* leaving for work the previous morning.

She felt no apprehension as she stepped off the elevator onto Fridge's floor. The waiting was over. She didn't need—or want—any more time to vanquish her fears. At long last, she was ready, ready, more than ready to accept the proposal of the man she loved.

"Hi, Keezia," one of the nurses greeted her.

"Hey, Sharyn," Keezia returned, noticing that the nursing station apparently had a new clerk. She was a bosomy young black woman who looked vaguely familiar. Under normal circumstances, Keezia would have driven herself crazy trying to remember where she might have seen her. But these were not normal circumstances. "Is Fridge back from physical therapy yet?"

"Actually—" Sharyn frowned "—he didn't go this morning."

Keezia's heart skipped a beat. Maybe two. "Is something wrong?"

"I don't think so." The nurse gestured. "I mean, all his vital signs were fine. The burns and grafts seem to be healing nicely. He said he didn't feel like going. I called Dr. Weston. He decided it was okay to let the session slide, just this once."

"So—" She needed a summation.

"So, it's no big deal. Fridge seems a little down, though. Maybe you can think of something to cheer him up."

Keezia drew herself erect and lifted her chin. "Maybe I can," she agreed, and headed down the hall.

Fridge was propped up in bed, apparently lost in thought, when she entered his room. Although he looked much as he had at Phoebe and Jackson's wedding, there was a slightly unsettling quality to his repose.

"Fridge?" she asked softly.

He blinked several times, then turned his head to look at her. His gaze flicked down her body and back up. Something in his expression told her he'd recognized the jumpsuit.

"Hey," he replied, barely inflecting the word.

She moved to the side of the bed, tangentially observing

that the baskets of flowers she'd arranged for Phoebe and Jackson's wedding had been removed. She also noticed a large stack of unopened mail on the bedside stand.

"Nurse Crumley said you didn't go to physical therapy this morning."

"Didn't much feel like it."

She stroked his right upper arm. "You really should go."

"Tomorrow." He shrugged, his broad shoulders straining against his pajama tops.

"Fridge—"

"What's up with you?" he interrupted, fixing her with a dark, steady gaze. It was plain he'd said all that he was going to say about skipping his physical therapy.

"M-me?" She winced inwardly at the stammer. "Well, actually…I want to talk."

"About?"

"Us." She moistened her lips. "You and me."

"What about us?"

Fridge shifted his position as he asked the question. Keezia had the feeling that he thought he knew what she was going to say and was bracing himself against it. Her first impulse was to plunge straight to the point and tell him that she was ready to accept his proposal and wanted to marry him as soon as possible. She quelled this impulse, however, recognizing that she needed to build up to announcing her change of heart. Taking a deep breath, she began to lay the foundation for her revelation.

"We haven't really talked about the night you were hurt," she observed. "You know Phoebe and I were out together. We'd gone to a movie and we were having dessert at a café in Buckhead. There was a big-screen TV behind the bar. The eleven o'clock news came on and the first story was about a fire. I happened to look over and saw the scene. At first I didn't know what was going on, because the sound was turned down. Then I—" her throat tightened as she relived with hideous clarity the moment when she'd recognized the fire site "—I realized that the burning building was a warehouse in our zone. I yelled for someone to turn up the sound on the

TV. The next thing I heard was that there were three firefighters confirmed dead and two more seriously injured.''

"So you and Phoebe went tearin' off to the scene."

"To find out about you and Jackson." Keezia closed her eyes for a moment. "When Sam Fields told me about the explosion...about you being taken away in an ambulance..."

Fridge made a sound. It might have been an aborted attempt to say her name. It might have been a groan of pain. Keezia opened her eyes and looked at him uncertainly.

"Fridge?" she prompted after a moment.

"Nothin'." He shook his head, his expression impossible to read.

It wasn't nothing and she knew it. But what it was, she couldn't say.

"I was so...scared," she resumed, watching him closely. She saw his eyes flicker at her choice of adjective. "Dear God, if something had happened to you—"

"Somethin' did happen to me."

"I know that," she said quickly, stiffening at his tone. "I know you were hurt. But what I meant was, if you hadn't... m-made it..."

"Like Dwight Daniels."

"Yes." Or Mitch Jones. Or Calvin Lee, the third firefighter who'd been killed in the warehouse blaze. "I honestly don't know what I would have done, Fridge."

His gaze slid away from hers. "You're a strong woman," he said after several seconds, his voice curiously flat. "You would have done just fine."

"I'm not sure I would've wanted to."

Brown eyes returned to topaz ones. "What are you tryin' to say?"

"That I love you, Fridge. I've loved you for a long time. But I didn't understand how much—or how well—until I faced up to the possibility of losing you. Really, truly losing you. Forever. And when I confronted that possibility, I realized what a coward I've been. That...time...I've kept asking you for? I don't need any more of it. I know what I want."

"Which is?"

"To marry you," she said simply. "To be your wife. To make a home and have a family with you."

There was a long silence. Keezia's pulse accelerated, then began to pound. She clenched and unclenched her hands, anxiously studying her lover's striking, dark-skinned face. Why didn't he respond? she wondered. Was what she'd said so...unexpected?

"F-Fridge?" she finally prompted, her breath hitching in her throat.

"What kind of fool do you take me for?" he asked. His voice was soft, almost silken. The expression in his eyes was not.

Keezia went cold. A tremor shook her. "What?"

"What kind of fool do you take me for?" He repeated the question through gritted teeth.

"I don't—"

"You wouldn't have me for a husband when I was whole. But now that I'm burned up and broken down, you're more than ready to marry me."

"No!" She was so shocked by his assessment of the situation, she could barely force the word out.

"You don't have to be afraid of me anymore, do you?" he went on, ignoring her protest. "That's the down-and-dirty truth, isn't it? The way I am, you don't have to be afraid at all."

"I wasn't—"

"Yes, you were." He practically spat out the words. "And if I were standin' on my own two feet right now, you'd be afraid again. But I'm not standin' by myself and we both know it may be a long, long time before I am. So you can afford to be courageous, can't you?" He shook his head, his face hard. "You say what you feel for me is love. Well, what I see—what I hear—is *pity*. And whole or hurt, pity's not what I want from a wife."

"I don't pity you!" Had her heart not been breaking, Keezia would have laughed at the idea. It was that ridiculous. "I could *never* pity you."

But the man she loved didn't believe her. She could see it in his eyes.

"I asked you to marry me three times," he reminded her, his voice bitter. "*Three times!* Why is it you couldn't bring yourself to say yes until I was flat on my goddamned back in a goddamned hospital?"

"*I don't know!*" The answer came geysering out of her, fueled by a jumble of emotions she couldn't begin to sort through.

There was a disastrous silence. Finally Ralph Booker Randall said very quietly, "Maybe you'd better find out, Keezia Lorraine. Because until you do, until you can explain your thinkin' to me—*to yourself*—I don't want to see you again."

Eleven

Keezia kept her head up and her back straight as she walked—not ran—from Fridge's hospital room. She maintained the same posture, the same deliberate pace, as she made her way to the ladies' room down the hall. But once inside the lavatory, she dashed into the same stall where Phoebe Donovan had nearly piddled away her wedding day and was violently ill.

The retching went on for a long time. Her stomach would no sooner start to settle than she'd remember a fragment of the encounter she'd just endured and start vomiting again.

Fridge, demanding to know what kind of fool she took him for...

Fridge, accusing her of accepting his marriage proposal out of pity...

Fridge, telling her that he didn't want to see her again until he figured out why she'd done what she'd done...

Finally, the sickness passed. Keezia staggered out of the stall and over to a row of sinks on the opposite wall. She turned on the taps and splashed water on her clammy face.

Turning off the taps, she fumbled for and found some pape
towels. They felt harsh against her face as she used them t
blot up the moisture clinging to her forehead, cheeks and chin

There was a long, water-spotted mirror hanging above th
sinks. After discarding the crumpled towels, Keezia stared int
it. The face reflected back at her was wan and miserable
looking. As it wavered in and out of focus. she found hersel
recalling something she'd confided to Phoebe the night of th
warehouse fire that had altered so many lives.

*"I bought into everything Tyrell laid on me for nearly thre
years,"* she'd confessed. *"Including the idea that his beatin
me was my fault. Then one morning I looked into the bathroo
mirror and saw a woman I didn't recognize. She had a blac
eye and a split lip and she was wearing the kind of expressio
you usually see in zombie movies. After a few seconds, I re
alized that this woman—this stranger—was me. And, well, I'
not certain how to explain what happened next. But all of
sudden, this little voice inside me started saying, 'This isn
right, girl. You haven't done anything to deserve this. Even
you're as worthless as Tyrell keeps telling you—which yo
know in your soul you aren't—you do not—deserve to b
treated this way.'"*

Keezia inhaled shakily, praying for that little voice to spea
to her again. To offer her counsel in this moment of emotion:
crisis. But the little voice remained stubbornly silent. Instea
her brain replayed another piece of her scene with Fridge.

"I asked you to marry me three times," he'd reminded he
*"Three times! Why is it you couldn't bring yourself to say y
until I was flat on my goddamned back in a goddamned ho.
pital?"*

Keezia closed her eyes, grappling with the implications
the almost involuntary admission of ignorance she'd made
response to this angry, uncharacteristically profane questio
Why had she held back from accepting Fridge's proposal f
so long? she demanded of herself. She'd found the courage
turn away from Tyrell Babcock and all he stood for. Why ha
she been so frightened of turning toward a man she knew
be good and—

"Uh...'scuse me," a feminine voice said hesitantly.

Keezia jerked, her eyelids popping open while her pulse took off like a startled jackrabbit. She pivoted unsteadily in the direction of the ladies' room door. Standing a few feet inside it was the new clerk from the nursing station—the one she'd thought looked vaguely familiar.

"Are you okay?" the busty young woman asked, lifting her left hand and patting at her intricate coiffure. Her talonlike nails were painted jade green and tipped with silver.

"I'm fine." Keezia lied, using the edge of one of the sinks to steady herself.

"You sure?"

"Positive." She nodded to underscore the point. "I just need a couple minutes to myself. But I appreciate your concern."

"No problem. And if there's anything I can do, just ask—okay? I'm Bernadine Wallace."

"Thanks," Keezia said vaguely as the young woman started to turn away. Then the name registered, triggering a series of mental images. *"Bernadine Wallace?"*

Bernadine pivoted back. "That's right."

"You went to a party for a retiring firefighter a few months ago?"

"Uh-huh." The younger woman nodded, an odd expression flickering across her face. "Mid-May. I was there with my brother, Melvin. He's an EMT."

"You...danced...with Fridge Randall."

Bernadine's well-glossed lips twisted. "I would've tried to do a whole lot more with the man if I'd the chance," she declared with disarming candor. "But the second I saw the two of you coupled up, I knew it wasn't going to happen."

Keezia went still, stunned by this artless assertion. "H-how—?"

"How could I know? By the way you looked at each other. It was hot, girl. And more than that. It was *connected.* You two just seemed to—to—oh, I don't know how to describe it, exactly. But even standing on the other side of the room, I could tell you two—'' she gestured expressively, her shiny nails flashing ''—fit.''

Keezia said nothing. She wasn't certain she could. A lump had formed in her throat.

''Anyway,'' Bernadine went on. ''I asked my brother if he knew who you were and he said sure, only not from any personal contact. Then he told me your name and that you were a firefighter. That *truly* impressed me.''

''It...*did?*'' Keezia managed.

The younger woman bobbed her head, her eyes shining with admiration. ''It takes some kind of courage to do what you do.''

It was meant as a compliment, of course. Given the circumstances, though, the choice of the word ''courage'' was an unfortunate one.

Keezia swallowed hard several times. The lump in her throat wouldn't budge. In fact, it seemed to be getting bigger and bigger. Her eyes began to sting. The bridge of her nose grew congested. She turned away, knowing she was on the verge of crying.

''Keezia?''

The question seemed to come from a long way off. She gestured weakly, hoping that Bernadine Wallace would back off and stay away.

But Bernadine of the braids and bicolored manicure didn't.

''Shhh,'' she soothed, enfolding Keezia in a gentle hug. ''I know it's hard, seeing your man hurt the way he is. But he'll get better. My brother says Fridge Randall's one of the best men he's ever known. That goodness will help him recover, guaranteed. And it seems like half the city of Atlanta's pullin' for him, too. The nurses tell me it's been like having a movie star on the floor, he gets so many packages and cards and visitors. You just *know* that kind of caring is gonna do some good. So it's gonna be all right. In the end...everything's gonna work out.''

The last vestige of Keezia's control shattered. As the hot, salty tears started to flow over her lower eyelids and down her cheeks, she realized that the words of comfort she'd just lis-

ened to were much like the ones she'd offered Fridge the
night he'd awoken from his semicoma.

She wondered, anguished, whether he'd had any more faith
in her optimistic predictions than she had in Bernadine Wal-
ace's.

Three days later, she was still wondering.

It was shortly after 11 a.m. Keezia was back in her Virginia
Highlands apartment after pulling two shifts—one regular, one
overtime—in a row. A part of her had desperately wanted to
volunteer for a third round-the-clock gig. She'd decided
against doing so because she'd realized that she simply wasn't
up to it. Using work as a buffer against her emotional pain
was acceptable if she maintained her professional standards.
But as soon as she felt herself slipping...

If she couldn't give the job one hundred percent, she would
stop doing it. Because anything less than one hundred percent
could have deadly consequences.

The knock on her front door came as she was grooming
Shabazz. She froze at the sound. Her cat, who'd been uncharacteristically tolerant of her fussing, took the opportunity
to escape.

"Who's there?" she called warily. She wasn't expecting
anyone.

"It's Phoebe!" a familiar voice answered.

Keezia laid down the small brush she'd been using, conscious that her fingertips were tingling from the silken feel of
Shabazz's marmalade-colored fur. Deciding to tend to her cat
probably had been a mistake, she acknowledged. All during
the process, she'd kept flashing on images of Fridge's hands.
Touching. Stroking. Petting. Her libido, which had seemed to
shut down in the wake of the accident, had reasserted itself.

"Just a sec!" she requested.

Actually, it was more like a minute—or two—before she
finally opened the door to admit her friend. She would have
liked to take longer, but she knew that doing so would raise
suspicions.

Keezia realized the instant she saw Phoebe's expression that

this was no casual call. Yet she forced herself to behave as
though it were. The newly wed Mrs. Jackson Miller played
along at first, parrying questions about her brief honeymoon
with wit and warmth. But once they were seated on the sofa
in the living room, she abandoned the act and turned serious.

"I know something's gone wrong between you and
Fridge," she said bluntly. "I dropped in on him at the hospital
a little while ago. I didn't stay long, because he made it very
clear that he didn't want company. One of the nurses on the
floor told me he's stopped taking physical therapy. She also
said you didn't visit yesterday or the day before that."

Keezia looked down at her hands. What the nurse had told
Phoebe was true. She hadn't been to the hospital in more than
forty-eight hours. She had, however, been in regular phone
contact with Bernadine Wallace.

"He doesn't want to see me," she finally responded, forcing
herself to meet her friend's gaze once again.

"But why?" Phoebe leaned forward. "As oblivious as I
was to just about everything except Jackson during our wedding, even *I* noticed the way you and Fridge were looking at
each other. If ever two people were—I mean, I tossed my
bouquet to you because it seemed—well, I thought—"

"I know," Keezia said painfully. "So...did I."

"Then what in Heaven's name happened?"

"Fridge didn't—?"

"Not a word."

Keezia looked down at her hands again. Then, after taking
a long, deep breath, she began to relate the disastrous turn of
events in Fridge's hospital room.

Her recitation was slow at first, full of hesitations and verbal
stumbles, but it became increasingly fluent as she went along.
By the end, the words were pouring out of her in an emotion-
laden torrent. She couldn't have stopped them if she'd wanted
to.

"I couldn't believe it," she finally concluded, spreading her
hands. "I stood there and I listened and I still couldn't believe
it. When Fridge accused me of accepting his proposal out of
pity—"

"That wasn't part of it?"

"No!" Keezia was appalled by the question. "Of course not!"

"You don't feel...sorry...for Fridge?"

"I feel sorry for what happened to him. But I don't *pity* him!"

"You're sure?" Phoebe had shifted into her professional mode. "It would be a very natural reaction, you know."

Keezia opened her mouth to deny the possibility. Then she stopped and forced herself to look deep within herself. Some of what she saw shook her.

"Maybe, a little," she eventually admitted, her voice tight and small. "At first. The shock of seeing him in the recovery room after he came out of surgery..." She paused, gnawing on her lower lip, wishing she could block out the memories. Finally she went on. "Okay. Yes. Fridge's getting hurt as badly as he did broke down a lot of barriers for me. It probably got me where I am—wanting to marry him—faster than I would have otherwise. But I would have reached this point eventually, Phoebe. I would have! I believe that with all my heart."

"Because you love him."

"Yes!"

"Do you think he loves you?"

"I don't know," Keezia said honestly, then gave a jagged little laugh. "Funny. I sound like you the night of the fire. Remember? When we talked over dinner?"

"I remember."

"It's kind of a turnaround, don't you think? From where we were then, to where we are now? You, being married to Jackson. Me, being—" she blinked against the needle prick of tears "—w-whatever I am with Fridge."

Phoebe regarded her without speaking for several moments. Then, quietly, "It almost didn't happen, Keezia."

She blinked again, telling herself she was not going to cry. "What?"

"My marrying Jackson. It almost didn't happen. We broke up a couple days after the warehouse fire."

"You broke up?"

"I didn't say anything because you were so preoccupied with Fridge," Phoebe explained hastily. "And once we got back together…"

"But—why? Why did you break up, even for a little while?"

"Because I was afraid, Keezia. My mother walked out on me when I was a child. My father suffered a fatal coronary right before my eyes. My fiancé was killed in a plane crash less than a week before our wedding. It seemed that everybody I loved, I lost. And in the aftermath of the warehouse fire, all I could focus on was the idea that it could have been Jackson who'd been killed or critically injured. I couldn't bear it. So when he surprised me by producing an engagement ring and popping the question, I said no. One thing led to another and he ended up calling me a coward and walking out."

"I had no idea," Keezia whispered, shocked.

Phoebe smiled crookedly. "You've had a lot on your mind."

"But still…" She chewed her lower lip for several seconds, suddenly remembering a scrap of gossip she'd picked up the day before. "I heard something at the station about Jackson getting a promotion and being reassigned to the fire academy. He did that for you?"

"For *us*. And for Lauralee. It turned out she'd been harboring a lot of fears about his firefighting, too."

Keezia took a couple of moments to consider the information she'd just been given. Finally she asked, "Would you have married Jackson if he'd stayed on the line?"

"Yes." The reply was simple but very, very certain.

"Did he come to you after you'd broken up? Or did you go to him?"

Phoebe cocked her head, considering. "We sort of met each other halfway."

There was a long pause. Finally Keezia said, "I'm not sure where halfway between Fridge and me is right now. But I know it isn't anyplace I've been the past two and a half days. I also know there's been plenty of times when Ralph Booker

Randall's gone way beyond the middle to give me what I needed.''

"So?"

"So—" she stood up, a sense of purpose suffusing her "—I'm going to go back to the hospital and try to return the favor."

And she did. But once she arrived there, she didn't go immediately to Fridge's room. She went instead to the hospital's small, interdenominational chapel and prayed.

Keezia knew the chapel well. She and Helen Rose Randall had spent a great many hours there during the first week after Fridge's accident.

While Fridge's mother had maintained an almost awesome degree of serenity during that week, she'd run the emotional gamut. She'd raged at God. Tried to bargain with Him. Humbled herself and pleaded with Him, too. And shortly after the dawn of the seventh day after the warehouse fire, she'd offered Him her tearful thanks for Fridge's return to consciousness.

"...Amen," she finally murmured, then got to her feet.

"I was hoping I might find you here, child," a distinctively mellifluous voice said.

Keezia turned. "Miz Helen Rose!"

"I was just up visiting Ralph."

"How is he?"

The older woman sighed. "Not good. He skipped his physical therapy again."

"I talked with Phoebe Donovan—"

"Jackson Miller's new wife?"

"Yes. She dropped in on Fridge this morning, then came to see me. She's worried, too."

Another sigh. Usually a font of energy, Fridge's mother looked utterly exhausted. "You and he—?"

"Not good, either, Miz Helen Rose. But I'm here to do something about it."

"What?"

Keezia spread her hands. "I'm trying to figure that out."

"This is a good place for figuring."

"This is a good place for a lot of things."

There was a pause.

"I'm not going to ask what happened between you and Ralph," the older woman finally said.

"I'm not sure I could explain if you did," Keezia responded truthfully. "That's one of the reasons I came here. To try to sort things out with myself...and with Fridge."

"He's afraid, you know." A hint of tears shimmered in Helen Rose Randall's eyes. "Whatever he's said or done, you have to remember that he's afraid. And he isn't used to that. He isn't used to being weak, either."

"Fridge isn't weak." The protest was immediate. Instinctive. "I know he's been hurt. And I know the doctors have told him he can't go back to firefighting. But that doesn't make him weak, Miz Helen Rose. Your son is one of the strongest people I've ever known. Not because he's six foot four and could probably bench press twice his weight if he really tried. But because he's good and caring and decent. He's been strong for all kinds of people in all kinds of ways. For those school-kids he teaches about safety. For the teenagers he counsels at church. For *me.* That's one of the reasons I love him so much. Because he's strong in his head and his heart and his soul. I know weak men. I was married to one for three years and it almost killed me. Fridge isn't like that. I'm not saying he's perfect. *But he isn't weak!"*

Keezia stopped speaking, slightly stunned by her own ve-hemence. Fridge's mother, on the other hand, seemed quite calm.

"If you feel so strongly for my son, child," she said quietly. "Why didn't you say yes the first time he proposed?"

It was back to the bottom line, Keezia realized with a jolt. Helen Rose Randall's question was simply a polite variation on the one Fridge had flung at her with such devastating effect three days ago.

"I asked you to marry me three times," he'd said. "Three times! *Why is it you couldn't bring yourself to say yes until I was flat on my goddamned back in a goddamned hospital?"*

Why.

Why?
WHY?
And then, very suddenly, Keezia knew.

Had she stormed into his hospital room a minute sooner than she did, Keezia would have caught him using the bedpan. As it was, she nearly collided with the orderly who'd assisted him through a ritual that had become more humiliating with each passing day.

"Mr. Randall don't want company!" the slightly built young man protested.

"No problem," she said without missing a beat. "I'm not."

"But—"

"We'll buzz if we need anything."

A moment later, the orderly was out in the hallway, the door shut firmly behind him.

Fridge levered himself up in a shaky movement, acutely conscious of a sudden speed-up in his pulse. He wasn't prepared for this.

"What—" he cleared his throat "—do you want, Keezia?"

She moved to the side of his bed. Her cheeks were flushed. Her eyes were shooting molten gold sparks. She looked beautiful, he thought, shifting his position. She also looked angry. Very, very angry. Probably as angry as he'd ever seen her get.

"I want to answer the question you asked me three says ago," she replied. "The one you said I had to figure out before you would see me again. So here goes. The reason I kept saying no to your proposals was that I was afraid. But not of you, Fridge. Never of you. Of *me*."

"I don't—"

"You remember my telling you that you were just about the only person on Earth who never tried to make me feel like what Tyrell did to me was my fault?" she swept on. "Well, I realized a few minutes ago that the main person blaming me for what had happened was me. Oh, sure, I talked about knowing that the abuse was Tyrell's doing. But deep down inside, I believed I was responsible. I believed there was something about me—something I said or did, or didn't say or do—that made my ex-husband hit me. What's more, I believed this 'something' would affect other men...even the kind, gentle, decent ones.''

Fridge's heart clenched as he absorbed the implications of what he'd just heard. ''Oh, Keezia...''

She held up her hand. It was trembling. ''There's more,'' she declared. ''The morning I finally walked out on Tyrell, I heard a voice inside my head telling me I didn't deserve to be beaten up. But what it never told me—what I never stopped to ask myself—was what I *did* deserve. I've finally done that. I deserve the best. Which, to my way of thinking, is you. The *real* you, though. Not this—this—self-pitying wuss you've been playing at the past few days. I don't know who the dude who's been skipping your physical therapy is, Fridge Randall, but I want him gone.''

''I can't go back to what I was, Keezia,'' he argued. Her characterization of his behavior stung even though he knew it was on the mark.

''Why not?''

''Because I'll never be a firefighter again.''

''And that's the be-all and end-all of who you think you are?''

''It's an important part.''

''It *was*. You were a great firefighter, Fridge. And I'm sorry with all my heart you won't be able to do it anymore. But that's how it is. You have to deal with it and move on. And I'll be with you every step of the way. Whatever you want to do. Or be. Wherever you want to go. I'll be there because I love you. I love you with all I have. With all I ever *will* have. And I expect you to love me back in exactly the same way.''

''Because you deserve the best.''

''Uh-huh.''

''And what do I deserve?''

''That's for you to decide.''

There was a long silence. Then, very slowly, Fridge reached for the call button that would summon a nurse.

''What was it you called me?'' he asked. ''A 'self-pitying wuss'?''

"Well—"

At that moment, the door swung open. About six people—all probable eavesdroppers—stumbled in. Among them were his mother and Bernadine Wallace.

"You buzzed?" one of the group asked.

"Uh-huh. That physical therapy session I missed this morning. Do you suppose I could get it rescheduled for this afternoon?"

"Is it…important?" someone else questioned.

Fridge held out his left hand to the woman he loved. She took it without hesitation, a smile blossoming on her mocha-skinned face. Their palms kissed. Their fingers intertwined.

"Oh, yeah," he said. "Because if I don't start working again, my wife-to-be might decide to kick my black butt from here to Memphis."

"No 'might' about it," Keezia retorted, then bent her head and kissed him full on the mouth.

Ralph Booker Randall and Keezia Lorraine Carew were married one month later before a joyous crowd of family members and friends. While the bride-to-be had been eager to wed immediately, her prospective husband had declared that he needed some time to prepare himself to say "I do." Recalling the patience the man she loved had shown her in the past, Keezia had assented to his proposed schedule without demur.

That the groom had made excellent use of their four-week engagement period was evidenced by the fact that he took his wedding vows standing up then capped the ceremony by sweeping his new wife into a passionate embrace.

The centerpiece of this embrace sparked considerable discussion at the reception. Indeed, the happy couple just happened to overhear one particularly appreciative exchange between fire officers J.T. Wilson and Bobby Robbins.

"Man, that was some kiss Fridge laid on Keezia," J.T. commented admiringly. "Hot stuff, huh?"

"Three alarms," Bobby affirmed, taking a swig of champagne. "Maybe more."

"What do you think?" Keezia Randall whispered, snuggling a little closer to her new husband.

Fridge grinned down at her, his teeth showing white beneath his mustache. The expression in his dark eyes was very tender, yet utterly confident.

"I think our love is a fire, sugar," he responded softly. "And there's not anythin'—or anybody—that's ever goin' to put it out."

* * * * *

Return to the Towers!

In March
New York Times bestselling author

NORA ROBERTS

brings us to the Calhouns' fabulous
Maine coast mansion and reveals the
tragic secrets hidden there for generations.

For all his degrees, Professor Max Quartermain has a
lot to learn about love—and luscious Lilah Calhoun is
just the woman to teach him. Ex-cop Holt Bradford is
as prickly as a thornbush—until Suzanna Calhoun's
special touch makes love blossom in his heart.
And all of them are caught in the race to solve
the generations-old mystery of a priceless
lost necklace...and a timeless love.

Lilah and Suzanna
THE
Calhoun Women

**A special 2-in-1 edition containing
FOR THE LOVE OF LILAH and
SUZANNA'S SURRENDER**

Available at your favorite retail outlet.

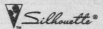

Look us up on-line at: http://www.romance.net

Take 4 bestselling love stories FREE

Plus get a FREE surprise gift!

Special Limited-time Offer

Mail to Silhouette Reader Service™

3010 Walden Avenue
P.O. Box 1867
Buffalo, N.Y. 14240-1867

YES! Please send me 4 free Silhouette Desire® novels and my free surprise gift. Then send me 6 brand-new novels every month, which I will receive months before they appear in bookstores. Bill me at the low price of $3.12 each plus 25¢ delivery and applicable sales tax, if any.* That's the complete price and a savings of over 10% off the cover prices—quite a bargain! I understand that accepting the books and gift places me under no obligation ever to buy any books. I can always return a shipment and cancel at any time. Even if I never buy another book from Silhouette, the 4 free books and the surprise gift are mine to keep forever.

225 SEN CF2R

Name	(PLEASE PRINT)
Address	Apt. No.
City	State	Zip

This offer is limited to one order per household and not valid to present Silhouette Desire® subscribers. *Terms and prices are subject to change without notice.
Sales tax applicable in N.Y.

UDES-696

©1990 Harlequin Enterprises Limited

BESTSELLING AUTHORS
IN THE SPOTLIGHT

.WE'RE SHINING THE SPOTLIGHT ON SIX OF OUR STARS!

Harlequin and Silhouette have selected stories from several of their bestselling authors to give you six sensational reads. These star-powered romances are bound to please!

THERE'S A PRICE TO PAY FOR STARDOM... AND IT'S LOW

$1.99 U.S.
$2.50 CAN.
Special Offer

As a special offer, these six outstanding books are available from Harlequin and Silhouette for only $1.99 in the U.S. and $2.50 in Canada. Watch for these titles:

At the Midnight Hour—Alicia Scott
Joshua and the Cowgirl—Sherryl Woods
Another Whirlwind Courtship—Barbara Boswell
Madeleine's Cowboy—Kristine Rolofson
Her Sister's Baby—Janice Kay Johnson
One and One Makes Three—Muriel Jensen

Available in March 1998
at your favorite retail outlet.

PBAIS

**Make a Valentine's date
for the premiere of**

◈ HARLEQUIN® **Movies**

starting February 14, 1998 with

Debbie Macomber's
This Matter of
Marriage

on

Just tune in to **The Movie Channel** the **second Saturday night** of every month at 9:00 p.m. EST to join us, and be swept away by the sheer thrill of romance brought to life. Watch for details of upcoming movies—in books, in your television viewing guide and in stores.

If you are not currently a subscriber to The Movie Channel, simply call your local cable or satellite provider for more details. Call today, and don't miss out on the romance!

*100% pure movies.
100% pure fun.*

HARLEQUIN™
Makes any time special.™

Harlequin is a trademark of Harlequin Enterprises Limited. The Movie Channel is a trademark of Showtime Networks, Inc., a Viacom Company.

An Alliance Production   HMBPA298

MONTANA Mavericks™

RETURN TO WHITEHORN

Silhouette's beloved **MONTANA MAVERICKS** returns with brand-new stories from your favorite authors! Welcome back to Whitehorn, Montana—a place where rich tales of passion and adventure are unfolding under the Big Sky. The new generation of Mavericks will leave you breathless!

Coming from Silhouette Special Edition®:

February 98: LETTER TO A LONESOME COWBOY by Jackie Merritt

March 98: WIFE MOST WANTED by Joan Elliott Pickart

May 98: A FATHER'S VOW by Myrna Temte

June 98: A HERO'S HOMECOMING by Laurie Paige

And don't miss these two very special additions to the Montana Mavericks saga:

MONTANA MAVERICKS WEDDINGS
by Diana Palmer, Ann Major and Susan Mallery
Short story collection available April 98

WILD WEST WIFE by Susan Mallery
Harlequin Historicals available July 98

Round up these great new stories
at your favorite retail outlet.

Silhouette®   Look us up on-line at: http://www.romance.net

SSEMMF-J

SILHOUETTE®

Desire®

M A N
of the
Month

1998

There is no sexier, stronger, more irresistible hero than Silhouette Desire's *Man of the Month*. And you'll find him steaming up the pages of a sensual and emotional love story written by the bestselling and most beloved authors in the genre.

Just look who's coming your way for the first half of 1998:

January #1117	**THE COWBOY STEALS A LADY** by Anne McAllister
February #1123	**THE BRENNAN BABY** by Barbara Boswell
March #1129	**A BABY IN HIS IN-BOX** by Jennifer Greene
April #1135	**THE SEDUCTION OF FIONA TALLCHIEF** by Cait London *(The Tallchiefs)*
May #1141	**THE PASSIONATE G-MAN** by Dixie Browning *(The Lawless Heirs)*

Man of the Month
only from

SILHOUETTE® *Desire®*

You can find us at your favorite retail outlet.

Look us up on-line at: http://www.romance.net   SDMOMJ-M

SANDRA STEFFEN

Continues the twelve-book series— 36 Hours—in February 1998 with Book Eight

MARRIAGE BY CONTRACT

Nurse Bethany Kent could think of only one man who could make her dream come true: Dr. Tony Petrocelli, the man who had helped her save the life of the infant she desperately wanted to adopt. As husband and wife, they could provide the abandoned baby with a loving home. But could they provide each other with more than just a convenient marriage?

For Tony and Bethany and *all* the residents of Grand Springs, Colorado, the storm-induced blackout was just the beginning of 36 Hours that changed *everything!* You won't want to miss a single book.

Available at your favorite retail outlet.

Look us up on-line at: http://www.romance.net   SC36HRS8

DIANA PALMER
ANN MAJOR
SUSAN MALLERY

RETURN TO WHITEHORN

In **April 1998** get ready to catch the bouquet. Join in the excitement as these bestselling authors lead us down the aisle with three heartwarming tales of love and matrimony in Big Sky country.

A very engaged lady is having second thoughts about her intended; a pregnant librarian is wooed by the town bad boy; a cowgirl meets up with her first love. Which Maverick will be the next one to get hitched?

Available in **April 1998.**

Silhouette's beloved **MONTANA MAVERICKS** returns in Special Edition and Harlequin Historicals starting in February 1998, with brand-new stories from your favorite authors.

Round up these great new stories at your favorite retail outlet.

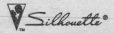

Look us up on-line at: http://www.romance.net

PSMMWEDS